A FEW WORDS FROM THE AUTHOR

They say it takes a village to bring up a child. In my experience, it takes a village of readers to hone a crime thriller. Big thanks to all the readers who gave me feedback on my draft, to editor Katharine D'Souza, and to my patient and supportive family. Thank you, too, for picking up this book – have a great time reading it!

A.A. Abbott

BY A.A. ABBOTT

Up In Smoke

After The Interview

The Bride's Trail

The Vodka Trail

The Grass Trail

*See **aaabbott.co.uk** for my blog, free short stories and more. Sign up for my newsletter to receive freebies.*

*Follow me on Twitter **@AAAbbottStories** and **Facebook**.*

THE GRASS TRAIL

by A.A. Abbott

Published by Perfect City Press.

ISBN 978-0-9929621-5-9

Contents

Chapter 1. SHAUN

Shaun focused on the pictures fixed to his scuffed white wall: ten photographs, almost identical. Blonde hair, voluptuous bosoms and green eyes beckoned. He would see her again, he told himself, and this time she wouldn't be pointing a gun at him. Licking his lips, he switched off the light and climbed, alone, into his bunk. Early though it was, he needed to sleep, to shake off the flu that was rocketing around the prison. A man in his position had to stay on top of his game. At least Bazza had been shipped out earlier; the bottom bunk was empty, and Bazza's snores would no longer disturb him.

Dreams came quickly, returning him to a familiar world: roulette wheels, sharp suits, flashes of fifty pound notes and flimsy dresses, the blonde blowing a perfect curl of cigarette smoke at him.

The grinding of a key in the lock and the clang of an opening door were simply part of his night-time fantasy at first. The heavies were throwing an irate punter out of the building. Shaun turned back to the blonde. Then, as his cell flooded with light and a screw's voice said, "Meet your new padmate," he snapped awake.

Despite the fever, it took seconds to recognise the man who strode into the tiny cell. He'd featured on TV news a lot recently, albeit clad in Savile Row's finest rather than the faded maroon tracksuit he was wearing now. The bald head and reddened, fleshy face were unmistakable.

With an expletive and a groan, Shaun swung himself out of bed. "A Tory MP?" he said contemptuously. "Do me a favour."

The screw, one of the older sort who thought he was a hard man, laughed in Shaun's face. "This isn't the Ritz, Halloran. You want a nice ensuite room to yourself, you shouldn't go around killing people." Evidently spotting the horrified expression on the MP's face, he added, "And you'd better not expect a hotel either, Jenner. You're in prison now. Get used to it."

The door slammed shut. Shaun's fellow prisoner composed his features into a rictus grin and held out his hand. "Marshall Jenner," he said.

Shaun took it reluctantly, delivering a bone-crushing grip. To his surprise, Jenner didn't flinch. Gradually, Shaun relaxed his hold. "A Tory MP," he repeated.

Jenner grimaced. "No longer. I resigned without compensation." His well-modulated voice was higher than Shaun remembered from the TV, and tinged with resentment. Another difference was Jenner's build: taller and bulkier than the cameras had suggested. Unlike Shaun, he'd made it over the six foot mark. He might even hold his own in a fight. Chances were, he'd have to; he'd be considered an easy mark by the other cons. A grim institution in an unlovely corner of south-east London, Belmarsh accommodated some of London's toughest villains, as well as Category A prisoners from the rest of England.

"Shaun Halloran's my name," Shaun said. "On the outside. Here, you can call me Al. Like the song."

Jenner's eyes twinkled at the mention of the eighties hit, causing Shaun to add aggressively, "No need to sing it."

It was clear that Jenner had no idea who Shaun was, which wasn't remarkable. Ordinary criminal activity was far less newsworthy than an MP fiddling his expenses for sessions with rent boys.

"Are you really in here for murder, er, Al?" Jenner ventured.

Shaun sucked his teeth. "You don't ask a man that kind of question when you hardly know him," he snarled. The MP had better learn about prison etiquette. "Actually, they put me away for driving offences."

"Oh dear," Jenner said, relief spreading across his face.

Shaun face-palmed. "What do you think?" he retorted. "Yes, I'm in for murder. The scum deserved it. I'd do it again if I had the chance, more painfully this time." Let Jenner stew on that. Perhaps the man would leave him alone now and let him sleep.

The former MP blinked. "I guessed it would be an activity of that nature," he replied. Although his high voice was strained, he still had a plum in his mouth. "You wouldn't end up in a Category A prison unless you'd done something serious. Then again, I didn't presume for a minute that I'd be coming to Belmarsh myself. I suppose I've been sent here 'pour encourager les autres'."

"Indeed," Shaun said, unwilling to acknowledge he hadn't the vaguest notion what his cellmate meant. Languages had held no interest for him at school. Even now, on the occasions he did business with foreigners, it was conducted in English. He coughed, a deep, throaty hack, which had

8

the satisfying effect of causing Jenner to edge away from him. "You talk too much." His temper was rising with his temperature, his head pounding in response to the televisions blaring through adjacent walls. The cell was a discordant battleground for different channels. Usually, he would have drowned the cacophony by switching on the old TV in the corner, but not today. Jenner wasn't going to either, if he had his way. "Make your bed and get that light off," he ordered the politician.

Jenner didn't argue. He spread his prison issue greying sheets and rough orange blanket across the thin mattress of the lower bunk.

Shaun heard thuds and creaks. "Keep the noise down," he said.

"I'm getting changed into pyjamas," his padmate protested.

"Do it quietly. And no flushing the bog in the night."

He expected complaints. Their toilet was inches from the foot of Jenner's bunk, although behind a plywood modesty screen.

Jenner didn't react. "Good night," he said, switching off the light.

There wasn't another peep from him. Shaun slipped back into oblivion, lost to the world until his cell door was opened at nine the next morning.

He'd been dreaming again, about his wife this time. Woken by the noise, he felt an immediate sense of loss, followed by disgust at seeing Jenner. Already dressed in his prison jogging suit, Jenner's chin bore the bloody signs of a recent shave with a dodgy prison razor. The disgraced politician, seated on a plastic chair, raised a plastic mug to him.

Jenner's hands were trembling, and he was bleary-eyed, but he tried to sound jaunty. "Good morning, Al. Can I make you a cuppa? Or anyway, what passes for tea in Belmarsh."

Shaun allowed himself to enjoy the moment before replying. A man who had been in line for a Cabinet post, socialised with the Queen at garden parties, was offering him a hot beverage in bed in a Belmarsh cell. Shaun almost warmed to his uninvited companion. "Later," he said. "There's just thirty minutes for exercise before you're banged up again." He stretched, pain flooding his head and body. It wasn't like him to sleep so late. Even so, he would have liked to have stayed in bed for longer. He added, "Haven't you got any better clothes? Only losers wear prison gear."

Jenner gawped. "Yes, but it's not exactly private in here, is it? I'd have to get changed in front of you."

"Suit yourself," Shaun said. With people to see in the exercise yard, he forced himself to move. He dragged a navy fleece and chinos over his pyjamas, shoved his feet into shoes, and retrieved the makings of a roll-up from his cupboard. "Coming?"

"I could do with a shower," Jenner said, yawning.

"Later," Shaun repeated. "By the way, the showers aren't private either. Here's a tip: don't bend down for the soap." He noted Jenner's jaw drop, and relented. "Just joking," he said. "I'm not a gay-basher and nor is anyone else. It's the twenty-first century. But cross me, and you're dead."

Jenner nodded, his mouth twitching. He seemed shell-shocked as he followed Shaun onto the landing outside the cell.

"Don't go jumping," Shaun said. "The screws would make me clean it up." They were on the second floor, right at the top of the house block. Their narrow landing overlooked a void, with a dizzying drop to the ground. A four foot high wire fence was no discouragement to a determined diver, and the wire safety net at first floor level offered scant protection. Still, the mesh was painted red, so bloodstains wouldn't show.

Another con nudged Shaun on his way past. "Going up in the world, Al?"

"Shut it, Jonesy," Shaun said, turning to Jenner to remind him, "We haven't got all day."

Jenner said nothing, staring at the stream of prisoners filing across the landing and clattering down the metal staircase to the yard.

"Keep your head down and follow me," Shaun said, rolling a cigarette and joining the end of the line. It moved at the speed of a lazy snail, as each inmate was frisked before going outside. "If anyone asks you for protection money, say you're paying it to me." He had no intention of shaking down the MP, but he enjoyed the flicker of alarm in Jenner's eyes.

"I'm broke, Al," Jenner protested.

"As if." Shaun shook his head. MPs' salaries were legalised robbery; everyone knew that. Anyway, Jenner had access to riches. "Your wife's minted. And she loves you dearly, doesn't she? She said so on the telly."

The MP's circumstances had been discussed in court and widely reported. Jenner, cash-strapped after a business failure, had made a good marriage. Jeannie was an heiress who kept him in style in a Hampstead mansion. She was clearly besotted, announcing tearfully that she forgave

Marshall's misdemeanours. Her love was unconditional, she had said; she had a wonderful husband who just happened to be gay, and she accepted that.

"Did you take a good look at my wife on TV?" Jenner complained. "She resembles a Rottweiler with lipstick. A fellow can only take so much."

"You're getting six months away, with good behaviour," Shaun observed. True, Jenner's wife was no oil painting, but the MP could lie back and think of his bank balance, surely? Shaun couldn't understand what might drive a man into the arms of a male prostitute. His own masculinity had never been in question, and for this reason, his reputation wouldn't suffer by associating with Jenner. He glared ferociously at anyone who looked in their direction, however. Waiting until they were in the yard and he could guide the MP to a corner, he said, "If you want to take care of your wife, I can put you in touch with people."

Jenner sprang back, stumbling a little. His face revealed disbelief. "A contract killing?" he asked, in a whisper so loud that Shaun briefly wanted to thump him. "No, that won't be necessary, thanks."

They were shuffling along the edge of the yard now, a stretch of concrete bounded by tall wire fences and their block's forbidding brick walls. Luckily, the comment failed to attract attention from the gaggle of prison officers gossiping together at the door. One or two cons looked interested until Shaun frowned and waved them away. He'd postpone business until later, or take care of it on Sunday in the prison chapel. Sweat prickled his face despite the chilly February air. He smoked wordlessly, the silence only punctuated by his coughs. A fine drizzle began to fall, and they were shepherded inside, to be locked in the cell once more.

Shaun was shivering and light-headed. He rolled another cigarette before remembering he'd had no food yet. Helping himself to Rice Krispies and long life milk from his breakfast pack, he switched on the kettle. A cuppa and a smoke would clear his mind. As usual, he'd be working as a wing cleaner today. Although his allotted tasks required minimal effort, the job made his commercial transactions easier. Where that was concerned, as was often the case, there were awkward conversations ahead. He'd be using an illicit mobile phone to find out why the last drugs parcel into Belmarsh was light, and there were debtors who needed reminding to pay.

11

"It was good to be out in the fresh air," Jenner said. "The smell in this cell was the first thing that hit me."

"Oh?" Shaun growled, on the defensive again. "What's that? I haven't noticed anything."

"Drains," Jenner replied. "And, er, tobacco."

"Suppose you're going to tell me smoking's bad for me?" Shaun jeered.

"You're obviously a clever man. I'm sure you've worked it out," Jenner said. He was calmer now, in the mood for small talk. "Have you been here long?"

"Just over a year," Shaun said. "I served a short sentence about twenty five years ago. Managed to stay out of trouble in between." At any rate, he hadn't been caught while he built his empire, graduating swiftly from the burglaries that had landed him in gaol in the first place. Drugs, drinking dens and bootlegging had propelled him into the big time, with a huge house in Wanstead and a monied lifestyle. For a split second, he recalled happier days: lounging in the large garden, drinking champagne and doing cocaine while his wife hosted parties for his friends.

That era had vanished forever with Meg's death, and later, the unfortunate events that had led to his current detention and the seizure of his property by a rapacious government. Whatever they'd done with the money, it hadn't been spent on Belmarsh. "Prisons have gone downhill," Shaun grumbled. "We're banged up for longer. The food was terrible in the old days, and now it's worse, as you'll discover if you haven't already. The old lags tell me I should blame your Tory cuts for that." He scowled.

"Then I'm suffering poetic justice," Jenner replied. "Can I ask if we had your vote?"

"I never vote. It only encourages you lot," Shaun said. As an entrepreneur, he had a certain affinity for Jenner's party, but he would have been more inclined to write his cross against UKIP had he bothered to stagger from pub to polling station. There were too many foreign gangs trying to muscle in on his territory. He believed the British should be running crime rackets in Britain; Eastern Europeans should sell their drugs back home and leave London to the locals. "I will say, we should get out of the EU as quickly as possible. Stop all that immigration," he opined.

12

"Oh, I couldn't agree more, Al," Jenner said. "If only I'm out for the Brexit vote. I'm appealing my sentence, so fingers crossed."

The kettle hissed, rocked, and jolted to a halt. "Want a brew?" Shaun offered.

"Please. Milk, one sugar." Jenner held out his plastic mug. "Thanks. Hot and wet; that's how I like it. Are you married, by the way?"

"No," Shaun replied. "My wife died a few years back." It was all he intended to say on the subject. He still missed Meg, and not a day went by that he didn't curse the cancer that had carried her away. Such thoughts, and his dry tears, he kept to himself. His survival and success depended on forbearing to show weakness. He added brusquely, "Of natural causes. And don't get any ideas. I'm strictly hetero." He didn't suppose Jenner had the nerve to make a pass at him, but it wasn't impossible for the MP to feel some attraction. Shaun's Irish heritage had blessed him with good looks; even pushing fifty, his now-grey hair was thick, his blue eyes large, his body trim and well-muscled. The paunch he'd developed on the outside was gone; he was back in shape at last, his muscles honed by the gym and judicious use of smuggled steroids.

"Of course," Jenner said soothingly. He pointed to the gallery of photographs on the wall. Torn from magazines and haphazardly fixed with blobs of toothpaste, their ragged edges were curling. "Who's that? Your girlfriend?"

Shaun sipped his tea. The sweetened breakfast cereal was beginning to boost his blood sugar. He felt less groggy. "No," he said, unwilling to be drawn any further. He would never admit to Jenner how he'd been charmed by Kat's looks and posh accent, had offered her a job in his unlicensed casino in the hope of knowing her better. It had all gone horribly wrong. She'd disappeared, and so had twenty thousand pounds from the gambling den. It had taken a wild goose chase to weird Cold War tunnels in Birmingham to establish the truth: Kat wasn't a thief. She'd seen Shaun kill the culprit, though, and had held a gun to his head in the tussle that followed. No one, least of all a woman, should have had that power over him. As if that wasn't enough, it had been her evidence that had sent him down. His lips tightened.

Jenner wouldn't stop. "Who is she?" he persisted. "A model? I'm sure I've seen her in the news. You know, you must have one, two, three – my goodness, ten pictures, all of the same woman."

"Forget it, okay?" Shaun snapped. Jenner really did talk too much. "She used to work for me. I'm looking forward to seeing her again." His eyes lingered on the picture showing the most cleavage. There was no doubt he'd enjoy a reunion with Kat. Finally, she'd see who was boss. The pleasure would be his alone, and all the sweeter for it.

Chapter 2. KAT

"Is that another wrinkle?" Debs asked, staring at her compact mirror under the harsh fluorescent light.

Kat scrutinised her colleague's face. "No," she lied, wondering if she'd also be paranoid about ageing when she was over thirty. Thank goodness she had more than four years to go. "Coming for a drink?"

"Got to get back for the babysitter," Debs said. "Ta ra a bit."

"Good night, Debs." Kat pulled a light leopard-print coat over her uniform. Her crimson shirt, black slacks and waistcoat were smart, but labelled her as an employee. Now, leaving the cramped backroom through its chipped swing doors, she looked like a player.

The casino was plush, tricked out in lucky red and gold, although its colours were hard to discern in the shadows that cloaked the room. Isolated pools of light marked out the gaming tables, the beckoning one-arm bandits and the spotlit bar: her favourite place to chill after a busy shift.

"My usual, Richie," she said, perching on a bar stool. A vodka martini would help her relax. It was affordable too. Prices were reasonable and the quality high to lure Birmingham's punters and get them in the mood to gamble.

"Right you are," Richie said with a grin. "It's on the house, Kat. I'm practising for National Kindness Day." The head bartender was a lanky black youth, universally loved by his workmates despite his avowed ambition to progress through the casino's management ranks.

Kat sipped her drink, feeling herself relax. One day, she would be a successful businesswoman rather than a croupier. She wouldn't have to don a coat for the right to sit at a bar. "It was hectic tonight, wasn't it?" she said, expecting a nod of sympathy rather than an answer.

"Sure was," Richie agreed. "Want a lift home on my motorbike? I've just got to meet a rep first. I tried to put him off by saying this was the only time I could manage, but he's dedicated."

"Treat them mean and keep them keen, Richie," Kat said. "Who does he work for?"

"Snow Mountain vodka. I'm sure we can arrange a little tasting if you want to indulge."

At the mention of the premium brand, Kat looked away. She didn't want Richie to see the tears that threatened to spill. Snow Mountain held too many memories. It had dominated her childhood in the former Soviet Union. Her father had owned the brand's distillery, and the family had lived next door in a bungalow built in Communist times for the factory manager. While only a toddler, she'd treated the factory almost like a playground. She recalled tapping tunes on empty bottles next to the production line. As a teenager, she'd expected to inherit it. Those dreams had vanished when her father was imprisoned and killed. Her inheritance, too, was lost; despite her best efforts, she'd failed to reclaim the vodka business.

"What's wrong, Kat?" Richie asked gently.

"Oh, me and Snow Mountain," she said. "I'd rather not remember."

"We've all overdone it some time," he told her. "Don't worry about it. Can I get you another?"

Kat hadn't noticed her glass was empty. She must have drunk the spirits as if they were lemonade. "Please," she said.

Richie made a conspicuous effort to change the subject. They were talking about the weather when he spotted their visitor. "Here's my man," he said, pointing.

The rep was a youngish fellow in a dark suit and tie, his thick, curly fair hair waxed into smartness. His face broke into a broad smile as he approached them. "Hello, stranger," he said to Kat.

She nodded, unable to return the smile, or even speak. It had been a decade since she'd seen Tim Bridges. He'd already been working for the family firm then, so it wasn't surprising that he was selling Snow Mountain now. His father, Marty, had distributed the brand across the globe since the fall of the Soviet Union.

"Ten years," Tim said. "I can't believe it's been so long."

It had been the Christmas before her father died, when he was imprisoned in Bazakistan but hoping to be freed. At the time, Kat was still counted a friend of the Bridges clan, spending school holidays with them. The following summer, that chapter in her life was over.

"You haven't changed at all," Tim said. "I knew you instantly. That long blonde hair, those green eyes…"

"You guys know each other, then?" Richie said.

Kat sensed he wanted more information. "It's complicated," she said.

Richie took the hint. "Before you start chatting up my customers, could we have our meeting, please?" he suggested.

Tim had the grace to look sheepish. "Of course," he said. "We'll talk later, Kat."

At almost midnight on a Monday evening, it was quiet. Richie, standing at one end of the bar with Tim seated beside him, rarely had to break away to serve anyone. Kat listened discreetly. Although to her colleagues she was merely a lowly croupier, she had plans to build a vodka brand to rival Snow Mountain.

Only her closest family and friends knew of her aspirations. Having taken a course in distilling, she was already experimenting with different recipes. A stainless steel liner ran up the chimney from her brother's basement laboratory to his flat three floors above: part of a DIY still, from which the initial results were pleasant. The spirit was smooth and clean. A few more tweaks to the recipe, and she'd have a commercial product.

She didn't trust Marty Bridges and had no evidence to suggest his son was any more dependable. Nevertheless, she found herself agreeing when Tim sat next to her and offered to buy another drink. Perhaps it was the way he made eye contact, when other men might have been ogling her breasts.

"Kat, are you sure?" Richie looked worried. "I thought I was giving you a lift in ten minutes."

"I'll get a cab," she said.

Richie shook his head, but mixed a drink for her anyway. He winked and waved as he left.

"So, what brings you to Birmingham?" Tim said. "I heard you were in London, engaged to some City hotshot." Unlike his younger siblings, he had hardly a trace of the local accent, and she recalled them teasing him about it. Marty had ribbed him too. Tim's voice was the product of an exclusive school. The entrance exam was notoriously difficult and he'd been the only Bridges child to pass it.

Kat wondered how much to tell him. "We split up," she said.

His blue eyes were inquisitive. "What are you doing now?"

"Working here as a croupier," she said. "I used to do it before I went to London, after I had to leave school suddenly. Because no one would pay the fees any more."

Bitterness tinged her words. Marty had paid for her boarding school to start with, when her father was thrown into prison. His support had stopped on her father's death, presumably because Marty had gathered there was no chance of any favours in return. At sixteen, she'd had to support herself with odd jobs while she trained as a croupier.

She couldn't be sure Tim would recollect the circumstances, but it seemed he did.

"The way Dad tells it, you virtually accused him of killing your parents," Tim said.

"He could have done more to save them," Kat said hotly. "If he'd threatened to stop selling Snow Mountain unless they were released, the Bazaki government would have had to listen. They needed foreign currency."

"Did they?" Tim said. "I mean, it was fifteen years or so since the Soviet Union fell. Dad said Bazakistan was short of foreign currency and food in the early days, but that eased off."

"Still, he could have made a difference," she protested. "Instead, he was quick enough to do business with Snow Mountain's new owner."

Tim shrugged. "I don't know the details," he said, "but I'd guess Dad thought nothing he did could bring your parents back to life. Anyway, your brother gets on fine with him. And you've had plenty of opportunities to bury the hatchet, haven't you?"

"Can we talk about something else?" Kat said, regretting her decision to stay. She hadn't even overheard anything interesting.

"Of course." Tim's eyes displayed sympathy. "What happened next?"

"I moved to a casino in London. I was always good at maths, and I considered making a living from gambling. I wasn't quite clever enough."

"I don't blame you," Tim said. "The house always wins."

"You can improve your odds," Kat pointed out. "My ex did well at online poker. He was an actuary, though."

"There you have it," Tim said. "Financiers in the City are the biggest gamblers of all, making bets with their shareholders' money." He shuddered. "I love London, but I wouldn't want to marry it. Anyway, welcome back to the Celestial City. Do you think you'll stay?"

"Who knows?" Kat said. "I'm living here because it's cheap. It's the only chance I have of building my own business." Her older brother didn't expect any rent from her; that alone made her vodka project possible.

Tim's eyes widened. For a fleeting moment, she realised how attractive they were, then dismissed the notion.

18

"Good for you," he said. "It's something I'd like to do myself. I'm thirty-two. I went into Dad's business at eighteen." He shrugged. "I had to. As the eldest son, it was expected of me. But I often think how different things would have been if I'd been allowed to go to university and decide for myself what to do with my life."

Kat couldn't see what his problem was. "Why didn't you?" she asked.

"Duty," Tim said. "And Dad's never set any store by education, because he left school at sixteen and it didn't do him any harm. At first, working for East West Bridges was fine. I became the sales director." He frowned. "But it's not a real director's role. I'm a rep, and I'm paid accordingly. Dad has a huge house in Wellington Road. I have a small flat further from the centre. He's got a Jag and I've got a Subaru. You can figure it out."

That was a familiar story. Others toiled, while Marty Bridges reaped the rewards. Kat's brother had a joint venture with him, and couldn't even afford to run a car. At least Tim Bridges was family. "You'll take over East West Bridges when Marty retires, won't you?" Kat asked.

"I hope it's soon." Tim's face darkened. "Because otherwise, I'm striking out on my own. No matter what."

Kat had a brainwave. It was as simple as it was clever, and she was amazed she hadn't thought of it before. Just as her father had used Marty as a distributor, she could become successful by working with a well-networked salesman – a man like Tim. With him on her side, she could steal market share from Snow Mountain. At last, she would have her revenge on Marty, hitting him where it hurt: his wallet.

"I may be able to help," she said. "How would you like to work with an emerging craft vodka brand? I bet you've got lots of contacts. You could be telling them about an alternative to Snow Mountain. In fact, you could start right now, when you're visiting customers like Richie. Marty doesn't need to know."

"Just as well, because Dad wouldn't be impressed," Tim said. "Tell me more about this new brand. Who's making it?"

"I am," Kat said, adding, "It's my heritage." She wasn't totally throwing caution to the winds. Although Marty Bridges might suspect she planned to compete with him, there was nothing he could do about it. She could afford to risk Tim relaying their conversation to his father.

Tim stared for a moment, then grinned "I could see you liked vodka when I walked through the door tonight, but I wasn't expecting this. Let's swap phone numbers. I'll give you a call." He looked at his watch. "Did I hear you say you needed a lift home? I can help out there."

"There's no need," Kat said. While she'd told him about her vodka, she didn't trust Tim enough to show him where she was making it. She'd based herself in a property that Marty owned and rented to her brother. Erik was pathetically grateful for the flat; he didn't want Marty to know she was both lodging there and had set up a still.

Tim rose to his feet. "I'll walk you to the taxi rank, anyhow," he said. He placed a hand lightly on her lower back as they left the club.

Safe in her taxi, Kat mused about that touch, his eyes, and the pang of desire that had surged through her. Ten years ago, Tim had seemed impossibly old. Now, the seven year age gap meant nothing. However, he was Marty Bridges' son. It must be the drink telling her he could be either a suitable life or business partner. In an instant, she regretted giving him her telephone number, and resolved to ignore his calls.

Chapter 3. ERIK

Erik awoke before dawn. For a moment, he lay in bed, listening to his lover's rhythmic breathing.

Amy's studio flat was on the top floor of a Victorian redbrick building in Birmingham's Jewellery Quarter. There was no view from the window set high into the sloping ceiling. Even the night sky was blanked out with a roller blind. A glimmer of moonlight around its edges revealed Amy, her face pale and surrounded by copper tresses. She looked like one of the pre-Raphaelite paintings in the local museum. Tenderly, Erik stroked her wavy hair. Then, abandoning Amy to her slumber, he leaped out of bed, stretching to the point where he just avoided bumping his head on the ceiling. At six foot, Erik had to be careful where he stood in the flat. When Marty Bridges had converted the attic space, he'd probably forgotten his tenants would be taller than he was.

The glossy leaves of young plants glinted in the dim light. These were darria shrubs: three in terracotta pots on Amy's bookshelves and another four on the coffee table. Erik watered them before taking a shower himself.

He washed quickly, shaving to banish the black stubble that had appeared overnight. Unfortunately, he had to pull on yesterday's clothes: underwear, jeans and a black sweatshirt. He would have preferred fresh garments, but they were marooned in his own apartment next door. Retrieving them meant disturbing his sister, who had worked a late shift yesterday.

As he locked the front door of Amy's studio behind him, he glanced across the landing. There was no sound from his flat.

It was larger than Amy's, with a snug bedchamber separate from the lounge. There had once been plenty of room for his few possessions. When he'd offered accommodation to his sister, he'd expected to share it with her. Instead, although his clothes remained in the wardrobe, Kat and her belongings occupied every other scrap of space.

There was no noise from the first floor apartments either as Erik descended the steep stairs towards them, continuing down to the open-plan office on the ground floor. There, more of the little shrubs were clustered on a windowsill. They were bursting with health but also more prone to drying. He could almost hear them drink as he applied his watering-can.

In his homeland of Bazakistan, the darria herb was famous for its rejuvenating effects. Now thirty-five, Erik had devoted his adult life to developing a cancer cure from it. He'd persuaded his parents to let him study pharmacology at Manchester University rather than chemical engineering, the degree that would have led to a career in distilling.

Darria, and in particular the chance to save lives, was his passion. For years, he'd worked at part-time jobs while extracting and testing the active ingredient from the herb. Finally, two years before, Marty, his friend, mentor and landlord, had offered him a business partnership. They would commercialise the drug together. Marty was paying for medics to run clinical trials, although he'd insisted they sell darria teabags as an anti-ageing aid to fund their research. In Erik's opinion, darria tea tasted disgusting. He brewed a cup of Assam and switched on his laptop.

He was eager to start work. All evening, while Amy was out with friends, he'd pored over reports of the clinical trials he'd commissioned, and he hadn't finished his task. Just as he'd expected, the results were looking good. Absorbed in his mission, he hardly noticed when a corner of the screen announced it was already 7.30. None of the freelances who rented desks in the office, most of them living in the flats above, would arrive until nine at the earliest. He used the office's chrome toaster and Nespresso machine to make breakfast for Amy, locking the door behind him before taking the meal upstairs to her.

She was beginning to stir, her blue eyes revealed as glazed and unfocused when he opened the blind. "I've got a headache," she complained. "I shouldn't go out with the girls on a school night."

"Coffee will help," Erik assured her.

"Thank you. I need all the help I can get. Today, I have to be on my best behaviour and put on my smartest business suit." She groaned. "I last wore it when I worked in the City of London. I hope it still fits."

"Of course it will," Erik said. "What's the occasion?"

"Marty told me at the last minute that we'll have an important visitor today." Amy worked with Marty too, although in a humbler position. While Erik was in partnership with their landlord to develop a cancer cure, Amy was the marketing manager for Snow Mountain vodka.

"Who?" Erik asked.

"The million dollar question," Amy said. She sat on the edge of the bed, her long legs dangling below the turquoise T-shirt that served as a nightdress. "It's Arystan Aliyev, I'm afraid. He's over from Bazakistan

22

on a business trip." Seeing Erik recoil, she added, "Maybe I shouldn't have said. I knew you hated the man. You told me he was involved in your father's death."

He turned troubled eyes to her. "I don't know for certain, but I've suspected it for years," he said. "Aliyev was the chief engineer at the Snow Mountain distillery. Out of the blue, my parents fell out with the government and ended up dead, while Aliyev took over Snow Mountain. It's too much of a coincidence."

"Marty's never breathed a word about it," Amy said.

"Why would he?" Erik said. "He thinks the same way, but if he wants to buy Snow Mountain vodka, he has to get it from Aliyev." While he liked his business partner, he was under no illusions. Marty's wealth came from distributing vodka; scruples had no place in that trading relationship.

"If you weren't here, Marty would probably bring Arystan round," Amy said. "He's already booked lunch in a restaurant in the JQ, just off St Paul's Square. He wants to take Arystan somewhere flash. After all, Marty's office isn't in palatial surroundings, is it? It's a concrete box in a crumbling industrial zone."

Amy was right. Leopold Passage and the redbrick streets around it were in the centre of a rapidly gentrifying area of Birmingham. The converted jewellery workshop was tastefully modernised, immaculate and trendy. Marty would undoubtedly love to show off to Aliyev, to say this was just a small part of his domain, yet look how perfect it was.

Erik frowned. "You'd better warn Marty to keep the man away from me, or it'll get messy." He wasn't inclined towards violence, but he could make an exception for Aliyev.

"Imagine if Kat met Arystan," Amy said. "She'd scratch his eyes out. And probably Marty's as well." She pulled a face. "Then you'll be in trouble, once Marty knows Kat's living here."

"I pay him rent, and it's up to me what I do with my flat," Erik said. Naturally, life would be easier if his sister and business partner could be friends. He comprehended why they disliked each other, however. They both had strong personalities. Each possessed an entrepreneurial spark; each was absolutely convinced that he or she alone was right.

"Kat needs to get a place of her own," Amy said. "My studio seemed huge when I moved in. Now you're virtually living here too, it's crowded." She squeezed his hand, before continuing, "I love having you around, but we need more room. And we had it until Kat commandeered your flat."

"I thought you enjoyed her company?" Erik was taken aback. Amy and Kat had always been best of friends, had indeed been flatmates in London.

"I do like Kat, but she's a freeloader," she said. "You wanted to help her when she split up with her boyfriend, but that was nearly a year ago. She's taking advantage of you now. She works in a casino most nights, so she could afford to pay rent."

"She's trying to start a business," Erik said. "That takes every penny she's got." He was relieved that his younger sister had found a purpose in life. After their parents had died, she'd drifted, seeming destined for an existence as a party girl and a plaything for rich men. "I'm sorry. I hadn't noticed there was a problem."

He kicked himself for that. His work had taken precedence over his relationships. Even so, Erik was sure Amy had never showed hostility towards his sister before, especially when Kat brought samples of her latest batch of vodka for Amy to try.

If anything, he'd sensed friction from Kat. She didn't seem impressed that Amy had a new job marketing Snow Mountain for Marty, thus enriching both him and the odious Arystan Aliyev.

Amy hadn't finished. "Even worse, I bet Marty will go ballistic once he sees what Kat's up to," she said. "The cellar's supposed to be your lab. Marty thinks you're synthesising herbal extracts down there…"

"Of course it's my lab. I occasionally do research there," Erik protested.

"But that's not all that's going on, and you know it." Amy's eyes showed her unease. "What will happen when Marty finds out?"

"He never visits the lab or my flat," Erik said. She had a point, though. He was risking the trust of the one man who believed in him.

Chapter 4. MARTY

As Marty's taxi parked alongside the restaurant in Ludgate Hill, he could see Arystan Aliyev seated outside with a female companion. The pavement was wide enough to provide a heated smoking area. Other groups were already lunching at some of the tables. Aliyev had a drink in one hand, a huge cigar in the other, and a grin on his face.

"I see Harry Aliyev hasn't wasted any time finding a lady friend," Marty observed drily. "That takes the heat off you, Amy." He glanced at his marketing manager.

"How bad can he be?" Amy said, frowning. "It's broad daylight and a business meeting."

"I've told you all about Harry," Marty said. "It's up to you whether you sit near him or not. If he hits on you, you can't say you weren't warned. Of course, he's always telling me the ladies love him." He suppressed a smile. "In that case, don't let me stop you."

Amy, uncharacteristically dressed in a tailored black trouser suit, fastened the top buttons of her blue shirt. "Prim enough?" she asked, as Marty leaped out of the cab and opened a door for her.

Marty suspected she could look after herself. At five foot ten, Amy towered over him. He didn't suppose for a moment that she'd be attracted to Aliyev. Thinking of his own bald head and spreading waistline, Marty wasn't sure whether the years had been kinder to him or Harry.

Marching ahead to greet Aliyev, Marty recalled that Harry had once been very handsome indeed. That had no doubt given the distiller a head start in developing his reputation as a womaniser. Now sixty years old, Aliyev's jowls were heavy, his skin blotchy and his hair thinning, but the habit remained.

He was also a tobacco addict, and he laid the cigar in an ashtray as he rose to embrace Marty. "You're late," he grumbled in Russian.

The hug was overpowering; Harry was taller and broader, and reeked of Romeo y Julieta. Marty extricated himself, recognising the young Bazaki woman next to his associate. Luminous with youth, blue-black hair cascading over her shoulders, she could have been Harry's granddaughter. A year before, on Marty's last visit to Bazakistan, she'd been introduced as a secretary.

"A pleasure to see you again, Inna," Marty said, sticking to Russian. He extended a hand.

She flashed a sultry glance from her sloe eyes, leaning forward to kiss his cheek. Noticing Harry grimace, Marty allowed her a quick peck, then stepped back without reciprocating. He couldn't deny that his business partner had good taste, but he wasn't interested in spoiling Harry's fun.

"How do you like our fair city?" he asked her, taking care not to gawp at the ample cleavage revealed when she unbuttoned her snow-white fur coat.

"I love London." Inna's smile was dazzling.

Marty stifled his laughter. Clearly, geography wasn't top of the list when Harry interviewed staff.

Amy, evidently catching a word here and there, said in English, "There's a Ludgate Hill in London, too. I used to walk past it every day."

Harry turned to her. In slow, strongly accented tones, he switched languages to match hers. "I am forgetting my manners. I see Marty brought a charming lady with him." He clasped Amy's right hand, bringing it to his lips instead of shaking it.

The old dog didn't miss a trick, Marty thought. "Amy's the new marketing manager for Snow Mountain." he said. "She's been working on ideas to extend your product range, and you need to meet her."

"For sure, I do," Harry said. "We will speak English now. There is much to talk about." He winked at Amy, seemingly reluctant to release her hand. She reddened.

"Let's go inside," Marty suggested, suspecting Amy's blushes arose from anger and she was about to slap Harry's face.

It transpired, however, that Harry was not the only smoker. Inna produced a packet of Davidoff. Apparently, Harry had bought them on the plane for her, almost certainly because they were the priciest brand on offer.

"We'll stay here to take the fresh air," Harry declared in his heavy accent. He looked around with approval. "I like the old buildings here. The Birmingham red brick is charming. It is far quieter than Ludgate Hill in London." He tutted. "That is full of cars, dirty and noisy."

"Too right," Marty said, although further down the hill there would be traffic jams in the rush hour. The council was digging up the city centre and sending buses on a mystery tour through the backstreets.

"We have St Paul's too," Amy said, gesturing at the handsome Georgian church nearby.

Marty was proud of his city, but even he wouldn't compare the jewellers' church with Wren's cathedral in London. "Moving swiftly on, how about a drink?" he asked.

Harry was helping Inna remove her coat, rendered unnecessary by the ferocious blast of air from the outdoor heaters. He murmured a few words to her in Russian before suggesting they ordered champagne.

"Not Snow Mountain vodka?" Amy asked, tongue in cheek.

"That's for the evening," Harry replied. "Although if you want it as an aperitif, I can help you out." He pulled a hip flask from his pocket.

Marty rapidly collared a waiter, an Italian lad dressed in the black shirt and trousers ubiquitous in fine dining establishments. A bottle of Laurent Perrier champagne was produced to short order. The boy opened it, and poured four full flutes without spilling a drop as the liquid bubbled to the top of each glass.

"Cheers," Marty said, slipping into the unoccupied seat on Harry's left so that Amy wouldn't have to. He sipped the crisp, appley fizz. It was little different from cider, he thought. A glass of that, or preferably real ale, would have slipped down just as well. Harry's choice was popular with the girls, however. Inna was all smiles, although it was clear she hardly understood a word of the conversation and couldn't read the menu. "I'll ask the waiter to bring the specialities of the house," Marty offered.

The lad chose platters of cured ham, cheese and olives, then steaks all round. Fortunately, there was bread to mop up the alcohol, which Harry and Inna were guzzling at an alarming rate. A second bottle of champagne was brought and opened almost silently, the boy applying a white cloth over the cork with a great deal of panache.

The meal would cost a pretty penny, more besides if the afternoon lengthened into evening and they made a night of it. Marty's wife would be unimpressed too. He'd have to recover lost Brownie points by buying a bunch of flowers and a bottle of fizz for Angela on the way home. Eating his perfectly cooked steak, sipping Laurent Perrier, he didn't care. Whatever his views on Harry's morals, the man was a priceless business contact. His happiness was paramount. Marty relaxed, loosening his blue silk tie.

He had come a long way, he reflected. When he was a child, living in the mean flats of Highgate, who would have predicted that he would be a self-made millionaire swigging champagne in the Jewellery Quarter? Of course, nobody but local foundry workers and artisans would have gone

27

drinking in the area in those days; it had been a solidly industrial zone resonant with the sound and smell of sizzling metals. The decorative old redbrick buildings of the Jewellery Quarter had escaped the demolition crews who had reshaped the city during his lifetime. They'd survived to be refurbished as chic apartments, offices and bars. His childhood home hadn't been so lucky. The low-rise flats had been pretty, painted in pale ice-cream colours, but they weren't practical dwelling-places. Shoddily constructed from concrete, plagued by damp, they were prime candidates for the wrecking ball. He remembered seeing them, shuttered and blinded, immediately before they were obliterated. His parents, decanted to a modern terrace half a mile away, weren't sorry to see them go.

For a moment, the old streets, hardships and friendships of his early years shimmered in Marty's mind before vanishing again. The poverty he'd experienced had spurred him to succeed. He wished his children had the same drive, the hunger he saw in Amy, Erik, and even Kat.

Amy was doing her best to engage Harry in conversation. "I'm told darria grows like a weed in Bazakistan," she said.

Harry laughed. "Yes, of course. Bazakistan is definitely the best place for darria. And all the old wives make tea out of it, hoping to recreate their youth." He put an arm around Inna's shoulder, drawing her closer to him.

"So it truly does have anti-ageing properties?" Amy asked.

"I guess so," Harry said. "My wife likes her darria tea." He sounded bored.

"I bet Inna drinks it," Marty joked. "She's really seventy-six."

Amy and Harry chucked. Marty felt a prickle of conscience at gaining laughs at Inna's expense. He poured her another glass as she simpered, her eyes uncomprehending.

"We must order more," Harry said, waving the empty bottle. "Marty, talking of darria, when are you going to buy a farm in Bazakistan?"

"Never," Marty said. "And you know it as well as I do. When I expressed an interest last year, it attracted the attention of Ken Khan and his terrorist mob. I don't want to be kidnapped again." Ironically, he owed his survival to Kat, his fellow hostage, but their shared experience hadn't made them any better disposed towards each other.

"Pah," Harry said dismissively. "Ken Khan is dead. The President has the situation firmly under control."

28

"How long for?" Marty said. "Anyway, I hear rumours that Khan is still alive." He forbore from pointing out that this was more than idle gossip. Erik had told him the Bazaki expatriate community in London were raising funds to arm Khan once more. Why would they part with hard cash for a dead man?

Harry shrugged. "Well, you're missing an opportunity. Land is so cheap in Bazakistan, I should buy a farm and start selling darria tea myself."

"I have a local supply in the UK," Marty said. He decided not to admit how limited it was. Harry's last comment was most likely a joke, but it highlighted how vulnerable Marty was to competition. Currently, Erik was growing the herb anywhere he could: on a friend's allotment, in his office and in his flat. Marty desperately needed to establish the darria tea business quickly and diversify his supply chain. He made a mental note to investigate farmland on sale in the rolling countryside around Birmingham.

"Our tea is getting media interest," Amy said.

"Very good," Harry said, reaching across the table to pat Amy's hand. He must have caught a glimpse of her outraged expression, or Marty's, for he then topped up her glass from the third bottle of champagne.

The young waiter cleared the plates away. "Desserts? Coffee?"

Marty nodded. The boy returned with a tray of tiramisu, cappuccinos and small glasses of limoncello. He gestured to the bright yellow liqueur. "On the house."

Inna beamed at him, to Harry's annoyance. "I hope you won't be tipping him," he huffed to Marty, as the lad's snake hips sashayed back inside.

Marty took no notice. He would ensure the bill was handed to him alone. "Time for another cigar?" he asked.

Both Harry and Inna lit their favoured brands of poison. "An excellent meal," Harry said, yawning.

Marty stared at St Paul's Church, gleaming white in the winter sunshine. A blonde girl in a leopard-print coat, pulled tight at the waist to reveal a perfect hourglass figure, was crossing the graveyard. Briskly, she walked down Ludgate Hill, towards him.

It was Kat. He was about to look away when their eyes met. Worse, he knew from the curl of her lip, the expression of complete contempt on her face, that she had seen Harry.

Harry noticed her too. "Katya!" he called.

She walked past without reacting.

"What's she doing here?" Harry asked.

"I don't know," Marty admitted. He was as surprised as Harry. "Visiting Erik, I suppose." He smiled expectantly at Amy.

"Yes," Amy confirmed, without elaborating further.

Harry leered. He was practically salivating. "She reminds me of someone I know well," he said, "although a long time ago, when she was sexy."

Marty couldn't resist. "Would that be your wife, you dirty old man?" he asked.

Harry chuckled. "You know how it is, Marty. You have one Russian blonde, you've had them all."

Kat, her pale hair streaming behind her as she marched down the hill, was out of earshot. Inna drew on a cigarette, oblivious to the banter around her. It was just Amy who posed any concern to Marty. She glanced sharply at him.

That glare was simply irritation with Harry, Marty told himself. Amy couldn't know the truth. Of the quartet around the table, only the men knew that Kat's mother was very much alive, and married to Harry. About to be plunged into poverty when her first husband died in prison, she'd chosen Harry Aliyev over her children. Harry had been crazy about her then, perhaps besotted enough to bribe the police to do their worst.

Erik and Kat, in England for their education, had been left to fend for themselves. Meanwhile, Maria Belova had become Marina Aliyeva.

That wasn't all. Thanks to his time in captivity, Marty knew that Marina Aliyeva had bankrolled the unsuccessful rebellion in Bazakistan and even had an affair with Ken Khan. That piece of information gave Marty leverage over Marina. He'd told her it was in a sealed envelope to be opened in the event of his death. She'd tried to incite Ken Khan to kill him, but that wouldn't happen again; she enjoyed her luxury lifestyle too much to risk Harry's wrath should he discover her treachery.

And what of Erik and Kat? The longer Marty kept the secret of their mother's survival, the more they'd hate him for withholding it. Marty pursed his lips. He couldn't bear to imagine Erik's devastation when he found out what she'd done.

Chapter 5. SHAUN

Shaun slopped a mop around the linoleum floor, stopping to roll a cigarette. Occasionally, he sprayed polish in the air. The scent made him seem industrious. It also served to disguise lingering smells from hooch his mates were brewing in a cupboard nearby. He had, in fact, liberated buckets and empty detergent containers for use in the process.

Ed Rothery walked by, key-chain jingling. He nodded to Shaun. "I'll be inspecting the showers later, Halloran. They'd better be sparkling."

Shaun grunted at the screw, but took the hint. Thirty minutes later, Rothery appeared in the shower room.

It was a concrete-lined room with several tiled cubicles for the weedy press-button showers. The half-doors weren't lockable. Had there been any homophobic bullying, Jenner really would have been advised not to drop the soap. Shaun had let it be known he wanted the politician left alone, though. It wouldn't do any harm to have a friend in high places one day.

Rothery let rip. "Call that clean? I've seen whore's knickers whiter than those tiles," he shouted at Shaun. "Do it again." His huge bulk loomed over Shaun like a badly dressed bouncer, his sandy curls adding yet another inch to his height.

"It's OK, Ed," Shaun whispered. "We're alone."

"Why didn't you say so before?" Rothery grumbled. He glanced over his shoulder. "I've left the stuff with Bartlett."

"What exactly?" Shaun asked.

"One mobie and two parcels this big," Rothery said. He wiggled his hands. "I don't look too closely." He glanced over his shoulder, rearranging his thin lips into the semblance of a smile. "Can you make sure I get the cash today, please, Al? It's the wife's birthday tomorrow."

"I'll see what I can do," Shaun said coldly. "Watch out for a text when you come off your shift." Mobile phones were forbidden within the confines of the prison. Rothery would have faced disciplinary proceedings for carrying his own, let alone the device he'd smuggled in for Shaun.

"It's a grand, right?" Rothery's left eye twitched.

"Five hundred. As you well know." What kind of present did the bent screw have in mind for his wife? Shaun hoped she was worth it.

"My mistake." Rothery knew better than to argue. It was easy money for him, a tax-free weekly supplement to his miserable wages. A thirty-something with a mortgage in London could undoubtedly use the extra. Shaun was surprised more of the screws weren't tempted.

Footsteps sounded on the landing. Rothery switched from supplicant to tyrant. "You should be quicker than this," he yelled.

"Yes, Gov," Shaun said.

"Is that Halloran you've got there?" A couple of prison officers marched in. "Indeed it is. Come along, fella, you've got visitors."

"I suppose you knew about this?" Rothery said, with a sneer worthy of an Oscar. "Get that equipment tidied away, and don't waste anyone's time, or I'll be filing a report."

Shaun bundled his mop and bucket into the cleaning cupboard, and joined another five lags on the slow route to the visiting hall. It seemed like miles: long brick corridors punctuated at frequent intervals by barred gates, all of which had to be unlocked by an officer to allow the prisoners through, then locked again afterwards.

There was the inevitable queue in the waiting room. Shaun handed his rolling tobacco, skins and matches to the screws on the desk. "Make sure you write down it's Golden Virginia," he told them. He wasn't having them switch his burn for a cheaper brand.

There was another line to join after that, as the prisoners were frisked before entering the visiting hall. Shaun raised his eyes to the ceiling, knowing he would also be patted down on exit. He didn't attempt any banter with the screws, as he might have done with the regular staff on his wing; it was easier to submit to the tiresome procedure.

At last he was given a blue bib to wear, marking him as an inmate. In the annals of history, one or two lucky cons had escaped from other prisons during family visits, and the authorities weren't about to let it happen at Fortress Belmarsh. Thus branded, Shaun was admitted to the hall. He reported to the supervising officer.

"Those two over there," the screw barked.

Shaun spotted his youngest child, Jon, thick black hair peeping out from a grey hoodie. The other half of the duo was ginger-bearded Vince, a family friend. Striding towards their table, Shaun forced Jon to stand for a hug.

Jon's pale skin flushed. He pouted, still a petulant youth for all that he was old enough to vote. "Dad," he muttered.

"You should know PDAs aren't cool – that's public displays of affection," Vince said.

"Since when were you the elder statesman?" Shaun said. "If I want your opinion, I'll ask for it." He immediately realised his tone had been too sharp. Although Vince was only twenty-four, he'd been an able lieutenant to Shaun, as he now was to Jon. Goodness knows, Jon needed some brawn on his side, maybe even some brains. He was just eighteen, skinny and wet behind the ears; running what remained of Shaun's firm was a big responsibility. "I haven't seen my sons for a month, Vince," Shaun added. "I thought Ben would be with you?"

Jon fidgeted. "He had to go to Germany, Dad. A personal appearance. Sorry I didn't mention it." He was shamefaced, and well he might be; he'd had every opportunity during Shaun's daily phone call, made from an illegal mobile rather than the tapped prison landlines.

"How much is he getting?" Shaun asked.

"A grand plus expenses," Jon said. "He's opening a computer shop. Cutting the ribbon, playing a demo game, giving a little speech. Don't know why they asked him; he can't speak German."

Shaun whistled. "My son, the gaming legend." Usually contemptuous of those who stayed on the right side of the law, he was in equal measure proud of and perplexed by his elder son's success. Ben did less work and earned more than most criminals he knew, and nobody was going to arrest him for it. "I don't pretend to understand this computer gaming lark. I thought it was something spotty teenagers did in their bedrooms when they couldn't get girlfriends."

"It's eSports," Jon said, which didn't explain anything.

"Competitive gaming for prize money," Vince clarified.

"He's a geek," Jon said, his words edged with disdain. "I could use more help, but he's not interested. Only this week, we had booze nicked from Jerry and Scott's lock-up. I told them to rent one somewhere else."

"It's those Romanians," Vince said darkly. "I went round to see a couple of people; put the frighteners on."

"You see?" Jon said. "Everything falls to me and Vince."

"Ben's never been a great fighter," Shaun pointed out. His elder son could hold his own, but it had been plain from an early age that violence wasn't for him; his heart wasn't in it. "He doesn't take any money from you, so what's the problem?"

"He's not in the real world." Jon sounded jealous, and that was the root of the problem. The young lad had always loved video games too, but he didn't have his older brother's skill. "He doesn't even have a girlfriend."

"Do you?" Shaun asked him.

"No," Jon said, "but I get enough."

"What he means," Vince said, "is that he has that little skaghead who looks after the gear he sends inside."

"Careful," Shaun said. "The screws can lip read. You should know better, Vince." He turned to Jon. "What does he mean, you're leaving my supplies with an addict?"

Jon's dark-fringed blue eyes, so like Shaun's that he could have been a mirror, reflected his father's anger. "Listen," he spat, "Carla isn't a risk. She's a single mum in one of the tower blocks in Woolwich. I chose her because I needed a place local to Belmarsh to hide my stash. We both get what we need. I give her a supply, so she's happy. The social workers haven't taken her kid away, because they think she's clean."

"On methadone, anyhow," Vince purred. "Those little bottles are piling up under her sink. Worth a few quid, too."

"Small beer," Shaun said.

"I'm not selling them," Jon said. "Why take a chance for a pound a pop? Carla won't either."

"She's in love with him," Vince smirked. "Jon's her knight in shining armour."

"Yeah. She thinks she's my girlfriend," Jon said.

"All right," Shaun said. "I can live with it." In the end, it was little different from the deals he did himself when he wanted other prisoners to squirrel away his contraband. He could see Jon had made a smart move. His son needed a hiding place miles away from his rented flat in Tottenham. This arrangement was safer than a lock-up garage and came with more benefits.

Jon looked happier. "We bought you chocolate while we were waiting, Dad," he said, handing over a couple of bars of Dairy Milk. He pointed to the refreshment counter. "Cup of tea? I don't mind queuing."

"No, we've only got another twenty minutes," Shaun said. "Let's talk business."

"You have a chat with your dad, Jon. I'll get the tea," Vince offered. Strolling away to buy it, he cut a dash at the counter among the depressed mothers and wailing children. Taller than average, Vince appeared to add to his height in the way he carried himself. His ginger hair and beard were neatly trimmed, his clothing flamboyant: a white shirt, black trousers and red braces. During his work as a mixologist in Shaun's shebeen, alas long closed, Vince had sported similar attire. Shaun had assumed this was to look the part, but apparently not; Vince was simply a hipster, albeit with a tendency to mete out a beating when confronted with an argument.

"Ed brought your parcels today," Shaun said conversationally. "I haven't had a chance to check them yet."

"Mamba, skag, steroids – same as last week - and a Samsung," Jon replied. "Vince can pay him tomorrow. It's too risky for me to do it. The Old Bill's on my tail."

"How do you know?" Shaun asked, alarmed. "And if they're following you, why not Vince? He shares a flat with you, doesn't he?" The opulent family home in Wanstead had been seized under the Proceeds of Crime Act, as had every other asset the authorities could find: the nail bars, hairdressers, burger van, and buy to lets – and especially, the casino and drinking den in Tottenham where Vince had cheerfully mixed cocktails. It had been on a trading estate barely a mile from the chicken shop above which Jon and Vince now lived.

Jon shrugged, as if irritated. "I've been stopped a couple of times. I can tell I'm being followed too, and I've had to be careful. The car's too hot." He drove a cloned vehicle without insurance, as Shaun had always done. "I'm taking minicabs now. Vince never has any trouble, because he's officially living at his mum's." Clearly realising his father wasn't satisfied, he said, "I'll get Carla to meet Ed at the bus stop. She'll hide the dosh in her nappy bag, like she did when she gave him the gear."

Perhaps Shaun's body language revealed unease, for Jon added, "She knows what'll happen to her if it goes missing. It's five hundred, yeah?"

"Yes," Shaun said. "He wanted a grand, but he can whistle for it. Can she pay him today? It's his wife's birthday tomorrow."

Jon stared at him. "You going soft in your old age, or what?" he asked.

"Never you mind." Shaun wondered if his son was right. Ed Rothery ought to know his place. Still, Ed was a key player in his supply chain, and cunning with it. Try as he might, Shaun had never been able to obtain photographs of the screw handling the contraband that he brought into the prison. There was no chance of blackmailing Rothery; he had to be bought.

"I've been in touch with Anton, like you asked," Jon said. "He says the crop's not ready."

"That would be right," Shaun said. "He won't get the first crop until spring. Is he okay otherwise? No sign of the law on his tail?"

"No," Jon said. "I haven't helped them out by visiting him. Just phoned."

"Pay as you go?" Shaun had always carried a number of disposable phones on the outside; it was common practice.

"Yes," Jon said. "He's relaxed about PoCA. Says he bought the dope farm before I was born. No one can prove the money came from you. But," his face darkened, "Anton says, as that's the case, he should be getting more for his weed. Prices have gone up, it's risky being in touch with me, and Dunstable is too close to London. He thinks he won't stay under the radar of the other firms."

"That's rubbish," Shaun said. "If the old hippy can't stand the heat any more, he should get out of the kitchen. He's more trouble than he's worth, and so's his weed. It was a hassle for you selling it last year."

Jon shuddered. "I had to take risks."

"Right. And I don't want to bring it in here. With all the dip tests the screws do, it's easier to sell mamba and skag." These were substances that exited the body quicker than cannabis, and were therefore less likely to be found during the prison's random mandatory drug tests. Shaun despised the men who used them, but there was no better way to turn a profit. He wanted to teach the hippy a lesson, though. "Have Anton sign the land over to you, then sell it on."

"What about PoCA?" Jon asked.

"Okay, Vince, then. I want temptation removed from the old hippy's grasp. At the moment, there's nothing to stop Anton selling up himself."

Jon's concern was reasonable and Shaun was glad he'd raised it. It was a fact that Shaun's sons, their aunts, uncles and cousins were already under scrutiny, required to prove their assets were the fruits of honest toil. Regrettably, other than blood relatives, there were few individuals Shaun could trust. He still had a couple of bootleggers, Jerry and Scott, working for him, but their allegiance was increasingly questionable. In addition, if they were caught on one of their regular trips smuggling booze from Belgium, Customs would examine them with a microscope.

36

Vince was the obvious choice. He was almost a member of the family, yet unlikely to attract an investigation into his finances. His only convictions were for violence; the police wouldn't expect him to have access to large sums of money, and those expectations had been justified until now.

Their dialogue was interrupted by Vince. "Tea for three," Vince announced, plonking plastic cups on the table. He retrieved another chocolate bar from his pocket.

"I'll pass," Shaun said. He worked hard to stay trim, visiting the gym and buying protein rather than sweets to supplement Belmarsh's frugal menu.

"Mine, then," Jon said, holding out his hand.

Vince didn't react. Seemingly distracted, he waved at one of the other tables.

Marshall Jenner was just sliding into a seat opposite the redoubtable Jeannie. He almost jumped out of his skin, then waved back.

"He's late," Shaun said, thinking that was the disadvantage of the cushy job Jenner had found in the prison library. He was about to ask how Vince knew the MP anyway, before the answer presented itself: Vince blew a kiss in Jenner's direction.

Jon had noticed too. "That old bloke a friend of yours, Vince?" he scoffed. "Going blind, are you?"

"That," Shaun said icily, "is my padmate, Marshall Jenner, MP."

"You told me about him," Jon said. "How did you meet him, Vince - clubbing in Vauxhall? I thought you were seeing guys your own age."

From the sheepish expression on Vince's face, and the tabloid descriptions of rent boys snorting cocaine from twenty pound notes, Shaun had a shrewd idea. Was he losing his touch? How could he have failed to realise Vince was gay? They'd even worked together. Jon evidently knew. Of course, his son shared a flat with Vince. Was that all?

When he'd first been arrested for murder, his children's behaviour had given him cause to question if he'd ever really known them. It was only then, having dismissed them in his mind as idlers, that Shaun had discovered Ben was making money from his video games and Jon was eager to keep the Halloran criminal empire alive. It hadn't been easy for Jon either, with Vince alone displaying true loyalty and persuading others it might at least be advisable to present a façade of it.

37

Vince had stayed devoted to the family. Dismayed, Shaun wondered how devoted. Bile filled his throat. "If you touch my son..." he said thickly.

Jon jumped to his feet, his expression mutinous. "Dad, you're not thinking that, are you? Me and Vince?"

Vince laughed. "He's got a girlfriend."

"That's not what you both said earlier," Shaun pointed out. He exhaled deeply, still not reassured.

"Shaun, you're wrong," Vince said. "Jon's like a little brother to me."

"More use than my real brother," Jon mumbled.

More use than his father, too, perhaps. Still, hadn't Shaun been a good role model to the boys? He'd always displayed masculinity: a good provider to his family, a hard worker, and a ruthless opponent to those who crossed him.

Shaun looked away, afraid to make eye contact with Jon. He didn't have a problem with Vince's sexuality. It just wasn't what he wanted for his sons. All those years when he'd included young Vince in family parties; helped the lad's mother when her husband died in his last, poorly executed armed robbery; given Vince work – had it all been a mistake? His features took on a grim cast. "Goodbye," he said, reluctant to utter another word as the screws came to return him to his wing.

"Your time's up," one of them said.

It hadn't been quite half an hour, but Shaun wasn't minded to argue. He rose quickly from his chair and let them take him away.

Chapter 6. MARTY

March brought lighter mornings, but when Marty woke at 7am on the first Saturday of the month, he promptly turned over and went back to sleep. His lie-in was finally disturbed by the smell of frying bacon, a rare experience since his wife started watching his weight. His astonishment increased when Angela brought a tray to him. She must have been up and about for a while, applying the lotions and potions that melted away her forty-nine years. Her face was already painted, pretty in shades of pink that complemented her short blonde curls and sky blue sweater. She'd also had time to cook a full English breakfast. A large plate was heaped with three rashers, two lacy-edged fried eggs, a circle of black pudding and a hill of buttery mushrooms. Next to it stood a cup of milky coffee and a smaller plate holding two rounds of toast spread with marmalade.

"I've died and gone to heaven," Marty said, easing himself out of bed and into the pink plush chair next to it. He grabbed both handles of the tray, still not quite believing his wife would serve such a diet-buster. "To what do I owe the pleasure, bab?"

"Just building your strength up," Angela said. "Young Ryan's phoned in sick, and I wondered if you'd do the honours?"

Marty didn't have a clue what she meant. "Sorry?" he said, tackling the black pudding before she could change her mind.

"The gardener," Angela explained. "He's a lovely lad; very reliable until now. I've asked him to keep the garden tidy every week during the winter, and he's always turned up."

"I should think so," Marty said. "There can't have been much for him to do." Although their plot was about an acre, he'd never paid much attention to it, simply noting that nothing seemed to grow in the winter. His views on domestic duties were strictly traditional. He'd turn his hand to DIY if Angela asked him; otherwise, their house and its grounds were her domain.

"You'd be amazed how the weeds sprout when the weather's mild," Angela said. "Anyway, it's spring now, and the grass needs cutting again."

Marty tutted in a show of reluctance. "All right, bab. I'll spend the day on it, as you've asked so nicely," he conceded. Sunshine was streaming through the curtains. He was sure he'd enjoy riding his diesel-powered lawnmower and hacking at shrubs. It would be foolish to volunteer too eagerly, however. Far better for Angela to think the fried feast had won him over.

Marty whistled as he dressed in the comfortable old clothes he'd hidden at the back of the wardrobe to save them from being recycled. Fortified by more coffee, he headed outside. His tools were kept in a brick outhouse; higher quality lodgings than the ramshackle farm building where Ken Khan had caged him. Marty greased the mower blades. He was almost hoping that the engine would stutter and he would have an excuse to take the machine apart, but it started sweetly as usual.

After a pleasant hour riding around the lawn, Marty tidied the edges and hoed the handful of audacious weeds peeping through the soil of his flowerbeds. He admired his handiwork, drinking in the heady scent of new-mown grass.

Angela appeared with coffee and cookies. Marty eyed them in wonder. "Where do you keep the biscuits, then?"

She tapped her nose. "It's a secret. I like to have them when the girls come round."

"Not for your hard-working husband." He understood how it worked. Angela and her friends would deny themselves their Hobnobs until they had visitors, then succumb en masse to the guilty pleasure. Marty's relationship with food was less complicated.

"I just thought," Angela said, leaving Marty in no doubt that it was a command, "you could chop down any brambles at the back as well – I'm sure there will be a few."

"It's exhausting work," Marty said. "A couple more biscuits might help."

She fetched them without a murmur.

Anyone gazing at the garden from the rear of the house would see a large oblong of lawn, bordered by flowers and shrubs, with trees rising beyond. Scrutiny would reveal a wall behind the trees, with an arched gate opposite the house. Through this lay another plot, equal in size. Half of it was an orchard, and the rest had been left as a wilderness area. It had been an excellent playground for Marty's children when they were small and exuberant. The challenge now was to prevent the patch becoming too wild. Retrieving a strimmer from the outhouse, Marty opened the gate.

At first glance, he was delighted with Ryan's work. The fruit trees were tidily pruned. Looking through the orchard, there was no sign of waist-high weeds in the distance. Marty strode through the trees for a

40

closer look. To his relief, the nettles and brambles he expected had been completely cleared. There were tidy rows of a bright green, serrated-leaved plant. He recognised it instantly, not least because of the pungent smell. It was decades since he'd indulged, but he'd seen plenty of it meanwhile. It wasn't just darria that grew wild in Bazakistan. Erik's homeland was one of a handful of nations rumoured to be the birthplace of marijuana.

Alarm took hold. This surely wasn't Angela's little project. She'd never mentioned it. No, her talented young gardener had been secretly cultivating Class B drugs, putting Marty's liberty at risk. He bristled with indignation.

Inquisitively, he examined the plants for signs of buds and flowers. He saw none until he discovered a more mature clump underneath makeshift cloches fashioned from transparent plastic bottles. "Value Lemonade, two litres," he read.

A wild notion began to take hold. If darria and dope both originated in Bazakistan, didn't that mean they required similar conditions? Ryan's skills could be useful, as could this relatively unloved plot of land. Marty grinned, swinging his hoe. Building a rhythm, he blitzed the ground within an hour. Only the pop bottles were left. He lifted them.

The tiny green flowers called to him, evoking the Saturday night parties of his teenage years. In addition to strong cider, there had always been spliffs, a more sociable and grown-up version of the pass the parcel game he'd played as a child. Marty chuckled. It would be a shame to waste all the fruits of Ryan's labours. Like a naughty schoolboy, he took a quick look over his shoulder before harvesting the flowering tops of the female plants and placing them in his pocket.

He nearly forgot about them later, once Angela had left him slumped in front of the television for his fix of Saturday afternoon sport. She'd made him a pleasingly calorific plate of sandwiches, then gone to the gym with her friends. About to raid the fridge for a beer, Marty found the cannabis leaves in his pocket, and changed his plans.

He recalled that the leaves had to be dried, and smoked with tobacco. Switching on the oven, Marty drove to the nearest convenience store for Drum and Rizlas. He'd had enough exercise today.

Once he'd dried the leaves, Marty set to work constructing a joint. He laid the shrivelled greenery on a bed of rolling papers, heaping tobacco on top. Finally rolling the reefer into a cigar shape, Marty lit it on the gas hob and took a drag.

He coughed as the hot smoke caught his throat. Persisting manfully, Marty found an old saucer to catch the ash and settled back on the sofa, contented and drowsy. Even his team's poor football results couldn't dent his happiness.

Dusk had fallen by the time Angela returned. "Marty!"

He woke at the sound of his name, rubbing his eyes. The electric light seemed bright as the sun, sparkling with energy. He wanted only to lie on the sofa.

"Why were none of the lights on?" Angela asked. "What's that smell?"

"What smell?" Marty was genuinely puzzled. He tried to wave an arm at her, mildly perplexed when it didn't actually move. "Sit down, bab. You hurry too much."

Angela didn't appear impressed. Her eyes glared like twin blue lamps, her lips curving in disapproval. "Martyn Bridges, you've been smoking whacky baccy."

Had he? Marty rubbed his eyes, spotting the dog-end in the saucer on the coffee table and realising it was responsible for his condition. "That gardener, Ray or whatever's he's called, has been growing it round the back."

"Ryan - that nice young lad?" Angela said, shocked. "The cheeky monkey. I felt sorry for him, and he seemed levelheaded. I'm going to ring him now and tell him not to bother coming back." She removed her phone from her handbag. "Incidentally," she pointed an accusing finger, "you should have more sense too. You didn't need to sample it."

Marty tried to look innocent. "I wasn't going to make a fuss without being sure," he managed.

Angela laughed, shaking her head. "Looks like you've proved it."

As she began tapping at her phone, Marty recalled his earlier excitement, his certainty that his darria supply problems were over. He'd had a brilliant idea, and he must tell Angela. If only he could remember what it was.

Chapter 7. **KAT**

Opening the door to the basement below 3, Leopold Passage, Kat was assailed by the smell of a chip shop. Two demijohns resting on a scrubbed wooden lab bench contained a boozy, sweetish potato soup. The mixture was still fermenting. A third demijohn was half full of a very rough spirit, almost moonshine. Kat had made this by heating a tank of the soup just enough to allow alcohol to evaporate. Travelling up a thin pipe to a glass sphere above, the alcohol had condensed to a liquid again.

Unlike Snow Mountain, this was no factory filled with shiny tanks and scurrying staff. As the sole distiller, Kat was cook, engineer, chemist and taster. She'd had to boil countless pans of mashed potato, rig the kit together, run it, and taste the distillate.

Of course, the initial processes produced a spirit that was sharp, impure and unsaleable. It needed further distilling, and that was her task this morning.

Donning a white lab coat, she used another pipe to connect the third demijohn to a copper cylinder resting on the floor beside an old fireplace. Flicking a switch, she began heating the liquid that had drained into her makeshift still. The alcohol would be collected once more, then distilled again.

The third distillation was the most complicated part of vodka production, but also the most rewarding. The spirit was heated in a vessel in the old fireplace itself, then sent through a stainless steel liner all the way up the chimney to a series of vessels in Erik's flat on the top floor.

Kat was so absorbed in her mission that the morning slipped away. As a distant clock struck noon, she reached the final stage. She rushed upstairs, past the ground floor offices and first floor flats, to Erik's attic home.

The liner, a flexible pipe about four inches across, emerged from the floor at the rear of the lounge. Here, a chimney breast had been removed to create more space, enabling Kat to lift a floorboard and expose the flue beneath. As before, alcohol was collected in a glass jar, which in this case was held in place with a tripod. The jar was connected to two glass pipes. One, very thin and short, was stoppered with a plastic plug. The other ran downwards into a large plastic bottle.

As Kat watched, clear liquid dripped into the jar. This, the first part of the batch, was the heads: mostly poisonous methanol. It flowed away into the bottle.

After a few minutes, Kat knew the hearts would have arrived. This was her prize: the pure, clear vodka she wanted. Briefly, she removed the stopper, replacing it after collecting a few drops in a teacup. She dipped a finger into the fluid and licked it. Satisfied with the result, she deftly switched the heads pipe for another, sending the hearts into an empty Smirnoff bottle she'd cadged from Richie. Tasting every couple of minutes, she diverted the spirit into a plastic container once it began to taste sharp. This was the tails; not deadly like the heads, but unsuitable for drinking.

She could hardly contain her excitement. This batch had the potential to be her best vodka to date. Naturally, it needed time to mature. It was also too concentrated to drink, and highly flammable. She diluted it with distilled water.

Kat looked forward to giving her brother a first taste of the unaged spirit. Although both she and Erik had spent a large part of their lives in England, they appreciated premium vodka like all good Bazakis. Kat decanted a little of the hearts into a test tube for him.

Soon, she would have to go to work. Kat poured the heads and tails down the sink, collected pipes for sterilising, and returned to the basement. After switching off the equipment and tidying up, she removed her lab coat. There was no time for lunch. Running upstairs again, Kat changed into her uniform. A slick of lipstick and a mist of hairspray later, she dashed out of the building.

She was in a such a hurry that she didn't look at the screen when her phone rang, swiping blind before holding it to her ear.

"We speak at last." Tim's voice reminded Kat of the treacherous attraction she'd felt.

She shook her head. "I'm busy," she said.

"Oh, really? That's a shame," Tim replied. "I'd like to discuss that business proposition."

Kat's ambition overrode her doubts. "When?" she asked. "I'm just about to start work, but I can see you afterwards. It'll be close to the witching hour, but…"

"No problem," Tim said. "I'm working tonight. I'll drop by when I finish."

They agreed to meet at the casino. Kat raced back to the flat to collect two vials of vodka from previous batches. She decided to take yet another outfit with her, and threw it into her bag. Running late, she called a cab she could ill afford.

Her shift was so busy that she forgot about her impending meeting until she saw Tim at the bar. He was standing with his back to her, talking to Richie. It was only when Richie glanced in her direction, and Tim turned his head, that she gathered Marty's son had arrived early.

"Thirty minutes," she mouthed.

He sauntered to the roulette table, where the wheel was already spinning.

"Lucky red," he said, putting down twenty pounds' worth of chips.

The wheel slowed. The punters, a motley crew of different ages, genders and race, stared intently. Kat had eyes for Tim alone. She forced herself to focus on the wheel.

It settled on red seven, a popular number. On this occasion, the house was down. Tim took his winnings and winked. "See you at the bar," he said.

She'd chosen a plain black dress and jacket for their meeting, the kind of outfit that she recalled Amy wearing to work in an office in London.

"Going to a funeral?" Tim asked.

Kat laughed. "Cheeky," she said. "A vodka martini, please."

"It's already on the way," Tim replied. Richie proved him right a few seconds later, placing a cocktail glass in front of her on a frilly paper coaster.

"I've brought my product for you to taste," Kat said, fishing the tiny flasks of vodka from her bag. "Richie, can we have a clean glass, please?"

"Bringing in your own? You'll have me out of a job. Don't worry, I haven't seen anything," Richie said, handing over a schooner while pretending to look away.

"Try this one first," Kat urged, handing Tim a vial.

Tim poured its contents into the schooner. "Now, if I were my Dad, I wouldn't drink anything you gave me," he said, grinning. "It's no secret that you don't like him. But I think we're friends." He sniffed at the glass and sipped from it. "Smooth in both flavour and texture. Impressive."

"Better than Snow Mountain," Kat said.

He laughed. "I'd have to say it's as good as Snow Mountain. Don't forget who pays my bills."

"That was made with cane sugar," Kat said. "It's got a neutral taste. Now try the other." She gave him the taster.

Without being asked, Richie produced another glass. "Thanks," Tim said, tipping the liquor into it and taking a sip.

Kat watched as a rapt expression stole across Tim's face. "Like it?" she asked.

"Oh yes." Enthusiasm filled Tim's voice. "This one has a hint of pepper, yet it's creamy. And fiery, without burning. I'm guessing you used different raw materials?"

"Potatoes," Kat said. She'd needed a lot of them. Shuddering at the memory, she recalled cooking several large pans of King Edwards, only to see the Smirnoff bottle less than a quarter full. Composing herself, she said, "I've just amended the recipe, and I think it will be even better."

"Yes, I'm sure I can help you market it," Tim said. "Look, we need to talk some more. Let's have dinner tonight."

"At midnight?" Kat said. After a late shift, she'd usually go home, eat a slice of toast and crash out.

"I've been working all evening too," Tim said. "Come back to my flat. It takes minutes to prepare steak and salad. I'll drive you home afterwards."

Richie leaned forward, suddenly seeming much taller and less sunny than a second ago. "You treat her right, or you'll answer to me," the bar manager said. "And I know where to find you, Mr Snow Mountain."

Tim held his palms up. "You've got nothing to worry about, Richie."

Kat refrained from saying she could look after herself, and anyway, nothing about Tim suggested a psychopath. It didn't do any harm to have protective buddies. "You're sweet, Richie," she said.

"Ring me any time." Richie's brown eyes were soulful. "You've got my number. Wherever you are, I'll ride out there on my bike, okay?"

She smiled at him. "I will."

Tim's hand was on her waist again. This time, he led her to the carpark behind the casino, opening the passenger door of a gold Subaru BRZ.

"Uh huh," Kat said. "That is some Subaru." It was a sleek, sporty wedge of a car, its plate revealing it was less than six months old.

"It's not a Jag, although I like it." Tim brought the engine to life and accelerated through the backstreets and onto one of the main arteries out of the city. "That guy, Richie – is he a close friend of yours?"

Kat stifled a giggle. "Not that close," she admitted, risking, "Do you have a close friend in your life?" Whatever he said, she'd glean the truth from his flat. The tidiness, the décor, the presence of an extra toothbrush or indeed an extra person – relationships left clues.

"No," Tim said, without offering more information. There was a silence, which Kat didn't rush to fill, before he said, "We're nearly there."

Kat recognised Harborne High Street, a long row of boutiques and restaurants punctuated here and there by supermarkets. Before moving to London, she'd sublet a room in a block of council flats nearby. It had been cheap and cheerful, with a panoramic vista of the hills beyond the city. Tim's apartment, perhaps half a mile away, was very different. On the first floor of a low rise brown brick cuboid, it made up in exclusivity what it lacked in views. The small carpark was filled with models favoured by the aspirational middle classes: Golfs, Audis and Minis. Tim ignored the spaces that were dotted around, preferring to park in a garage at the rear. They walked across a perfectly manicured lawn to the lobby, then up polished stairs to his flat.

"It's a bit of a mess, I'm afraid," Tim said.

There were a few books scattered around, tomes on military history and the like. Other than that, there was little evidence that anyone lived here at all. The pale grey walls were unsullied. No dust had settled on the black leather sofa, light wood table and soft, deep pile cream carpets. There was no sign of another woman. Kat discreetly inspected the bathroom while Tim "rustled up supper." There was just one of everything she would have expected to see: shower gel, soap, razor, electric toothbrush. The room was poky, white and mis-named, with only a shower and no tub.

"I haven't offered you a drink," he called from the kitchen.

"Coffee is fine," Kat shouted back. This was strictly a business meeting, she told herself, returning to the lounge and examining Tim's bookshelves. She saw nothing to destroy her flourishing crush on him: no porn, terrorist manuals or evidence that he might be gay. Tim seemed to favour history, travel and action thriller writers like Lee Child and Rob Sinclair.

47

Tim appeared from his kitchen with a tray, placing it on a small dining table. The steaks were large, still smoking and surrounded by green leaves glistening with dressing. There was a white china mug of coffee for her and a bottle of Two Towers real ale for him.

"The first proper drink I've had all evening," he explained, pouring the golden liquid into a pint glass. "And it'll be the last, because I'm giving you a lift home. Now, tuck in." He gestured to her plate.

"Delicious," Kat said, appreciating each forkful. Her steak was perfectly cooked, tender and red in the middle. Casting her mind back a decade, she dimly recalled Tim spending time in the kitchen at Wellington Road. It had been a spacious, light-filled room, into which the Bridges family drifted whenever hunger assailed them. Lizzie, the housekeeper, had kept them supplied with cakes and snacks. By the look of Tim's athletic physique, the treats hadn't caused him to put on weight.

Kat wondered why a housekeeper had been necessary. It was a substantial dwelling, of course, and Marty doubtless didn't lift a finger, but surely his first wife could have managed the home without a full-time employee? Perhaps the bottle had been too tempting for her; she always seemed to have a drink in her hand, especially on that Christmas Day ten years ago. Not long afterwards, she'd died in a car crash. Recalling how Tim had also known tragedy, Kat regretted her earlier touchiness towards him.

"I'm glad you liked the vodka," she said, close enough to feel his allure but forcing herself to angle the conversation towards business.

"Yes, it's clean, with a creamy mouth feel," Tim said. "What's it called?" His gaze was expectant.

She hadn't thought of a name. Snow Mountain had dominated Kat's thoughts so much that she couldn't imagine a better brand. She wished she'd asked Amy for help. Erik had suggested it, and why not? Amy had been a loyal friend, and marketing was her area of expertise. What had stopped Kat was an edgy feeling around Amy, as if her brother's girlfriend was cooling towards her and even resented her presence.

"Go on," Tim said. He was laughing. "It isn't something rude like Wild Willy, is it?"

Kat realised she'd have to give him an answer. "Starshine," she improvised. She could change her mind later.

"A good choice." Tim nodded. "That has possibilities. You could have a clear bottle that turns into a starry pattern under ultraviolet light. That

48

would look great in a spotlit bar or nightclub." He sighed. "Anyway, I mustn't talk shop all evening. Where do you like to go outside of work?"

While her life in London had been a whirl of shopping and parties, Kat had very little time or money to spare nowadays. "Cocktails hit the spot," she said. "The Rose Villa Tavern does interesting things with vodka."

"When are you free?" Tim asked. "I'll buy you dinner and drinks there, then we can see a play afterwards. The Blue Orange Theatre is just down the road from the tavern. Have you been there?"

"Yes," Kat said, unwilling to admit she lived a stone's throw away from both venues. She added, "I'll check my diary."

He glanced down at the empty plates with a rueful expression. "Supper's finished. I'd better take you home. Unless you'd like a dessert?"

"No thanks." It was a shame that Tim hadn't wanted to discuss business for long, but even more disappointing that he hadn't made a move on her. Impulsively, Kat caught his gaze, holding it for a few seconds.

Tim smiled. He took her hand, pulling her towards him. "So you want to stay," he whispered, before kissing her lightly on the lips. "Did you like that?" he asked.

"Yes, and I like this too," Kat said, returning the kiss passionately and placing his hands on her breasts. She was used to men making the running, and she was bored with it. It was time for seduction on her own terms.

Tim squeezed gently, thrilling her. "Harder, Tim," Kat said. As his eyes widened, she added, "I haven't seen your bedroom yet." There were a number of doors she hadn't explored. She wasn't going to risk killing the magic by leading him into a broom cupboard.

"This way," Tim said, an arm around her shoulders. The room was square and dominated by a modern four-poster, airy with pale wood and white muslin.

Kat unzipped the black dress, stripping swiftly down to her underclothes. Beautifully crafted in ivory silk and lace, they were the last vestige of the luxuries she'd enjoyed with a rich fiancé.

Tim took off his jacket and shirt. He was removing his clothing at a more leisurely pace, ostensibly distracted by the sight of her. His gaze, heavy with desire, set her body tingling.

She stretched out on the big white bed. "I think you should remove my knickers with your teeth, Tim," she told him.

He obliged. Naked, there wasn't an ounce of fat on him. Kat's mind created an image of his father, bursting like a whale out of a dark business suit. She shivered, suddenly fearful. What if Tim couldn't be trusted, and told Marty about her business plans, or, worse, where she lived? She couldn't keep it a secret from Tim for much longer. Kat bit her lip, afraid she was playing with fire.

Tim misunderstood the violence of her reaction. "That really does it for you," he observed. He began to use his fingers, rolling the wispy panties down her thighs, stroking the moist area where they joined.

Her concerns vanished like nightmares in morning sunshine. Kat trembled with delight again. It had been many months since she'd had a lover, and her senses were heightened. Although she'd never had difficulty attracting men, she rarely found them enticing. Tim was different: charm, good looks and consideration wrapped together in a single package. If only he weren't Marty's son.

Tim kissed her lips softly again, until she freed her breasts from their silken cage, pulling his mouth towards them. Finally, Kat guided him inside her, moving her hips with his until her release came.

Chapter 8. ERIK

The silver Jaguar F-type coupé crunched over Marty's gravel drive, halting outside the porticoed entrance of his mansion. "I think you'll be excited by this," Marty said.

Erik was mystified. He'd seen Marty's dwelling, and its extensive grounds, many times. "What are you hiding? I don't believe in fairies or unicorns," he said.

"It's better than anything you can imagine," Marty said, sidestepping the question.

Marty unlocked the front door and called his wife's name. Angela emerged from the kitchen, wearing a dazzling white apron embroidered in pink with the words "Wine O'Clock."

As ever, Erik felt that Angela wore her years well. She must be about Marty's age, but looked a decade younger. Of course, she'd badgered Marty for a supply of darria tea as soon as she'd heard of it. Erik wondered if she could be persuaded to provide a testimonial.

"Erik, great to see you," Angela said. "Are you staying for dinner? Marty never tells me about his arrangements, but I can easily cook extra for you."

"Good idea," Marty agreed. "We'll need to serve wine and a pudding too, won't we? To look after our visitor." He beamed at Erik. "Angela makes an apple crumble to die for."

"What do you think, Erik?" Angela stood expectantly.

Erik accepted the offer with good grace, impressed at Marty's cunning in teasing a dessert from Angela. Her focus on calories was common knowledge among her husband's colleagues. No one doubted she had the best of intentions in nudging Marty towards a healthy diet, but he did his utmost to subvert them.

"I'll just show Erik the garden," Marty said, taking him through two airy, pastel-painted reception rooms and out via French doors.

The garden smelled fresh and green. A line of stepping stones in the lawn led to the blue gate at the back. Erik followed Marty to it, then beyond, past the little orchard to a patch of freshly cleared ground.

"You'll never guess what I found here," Marty said. "Our young gardener had a cannabis patch – without my knowledge, of course. Like darria, cannabis grows all over Bazakistan. So if we have someone who knows how to cultivate it, I bet he could produce darria too."

"He could, but why work with a lawbreaker?" Erik wasn't convinced. He scooped up a handful of earth with his hand, letting it run through his fingers. It was a rich loam, crumbly yet silken to the touch. He nodded. "Good soil. Darria would thrive on it. I wish I had time to start a few plants off here."

"I'm looking for a farm with soil like this, and a farmer as well, because your time isn't the only problem," Marty said. "I suspect Angela won't be pleased to see darria on this patch. I bet she thinks a single shrub will spread into a plantation and take over her garden."

Like a shadow, Angela appeared behind them. "You want to grow darria here?"

"At least it's legal," Marty murmured.

Angela took the bait. Her expression would have turned milk sour. "You're not turning my garden into a darria farm," she said. "Over my dead body."

Chapter 9. SHAUN

"Want a brew, Al?" Jenner asked.

"You're on, Jens." Shaun rolled a cigarette and stood next to the small barred window, opening it a few inches. Halfway through April, the weather was warmer, and courtesy cost nothing. Jenner didn't smoke, albeit he was buying as much tobacco as he could afford.

While they'd never be best buddies, the two cellmates were considerate towards each other. Jenner's sexual preferences were well-known and his occasional friendships with young smokers the subject of rumour, but he didn't flaunt them in front of Shaun. Shaun respected the politician for his efforts in helping less literate inmates with letters and forms. The MP had also learned exactly how Shaun liked his tea: strong, heavily sugared and whitened with a splash of milk saved from their breakfast packs.

Jenner gave him the drink. "Hark," the ex-MP said, cupping a hand to his ear.

"Singing," Shaun said. Through the open window, he heard a spirited rendition of Jerusalem, delivered in a sonorous baritone and loud bass.

"It's the Welshmen," Jenner said. "Cardiff Prison has gone non-smoking and they've applied for a transfer here."

"To Belmarsh?" Shaun was sceptical. "Why would anyone do that? Don't believe everything those screws in the library tell you."

Surprisingly, there was a grain of truth in the story, although like most gossip, reality was more complicated. Shaun discovered more during evening association, the two hour period permitted for socialising with other cons on the wing. He was on his way back from the dinner queue, happy to have secured an extra pasty, when he felt a tap on his shoulder.

Shaun spun around. "What do you want?" he growled.

The man who confronted him was a stranger, roughly the same height and build, but half his age: black-haired, round-faced and green-eyed, dressed in a prison tracksuit.

"Sorry," the lad said, revealing himself to be the baritone who had been singing earlier. "Jonesy tells me," he glanced at Geoff Jones, a middle-aged jewel thief, "that your padmate can help me out with some burn. I've just been transferred and the screws nicked it."

"Good stuff, was it?" Shaun asked.

"Cutter's Choice."

Shaun shrugged. He wasn't convinced prison officers would stoop so low. There were better brands to steal. Still, mistakes happened. The screws might have been having a laugh. They would know why the young man had been moved. "Come round later," he said.

"Right you are," the lad said. "I'm Tyler Williams."

"Al." He looked over at Jonesy, who was killing himself laughing. They would have words, Shaun decided.

The lad reappeared when they'd finished eating. Jenner was making himself useful, washing the plastic crockery and making another cup of tea. There was a knock on the door.

"Come in," Jenner trilled.

"It's our young Welsh friend," Shaun said.

"I say, what a splendid performance of Jerusalem," Jenner declared, looking Williams up and down. "It's almost worth going to prison for."

"Steady on," Shaun said.

"Thanks." Williams didn't react either to Jenner's patrician tones or the scrutiny. Perhaps he expected both. "I'm Tyler Williams. Just been moved from Cardiff. Need to borrow some burn. He said..."

"You didn't really request a transfer here so you could smoke, did you?" Shaun interrupted.

The Welshman looked embarrassed. "I tried to give up with the ban on the way, but it was impossible. I had to get a transfer."

Shaun understood this. He would have done the same. Smoking was the greatest pleasure of life inside. He occasionally indulged in hooch, or a selection of the drugs Ed brought into the prison for him, but nothing beat the reliable comfort of tobacco. "Why Belmarsh?" he asked. "It's a long way from home."

It seemed Williams couldn't fathom it either. "I haven't a clue," he said. "I told them I had a sister in Kent, so maybe that's the reason. Cardiff's B-Cat, and I thought I was in with a chance of a regrade on transfer, maybe strike lucky with an open prison, but I didn't expect this. You're A-Cat here, aren't you?"

"Exactly the same thing happened to me," Jenner said sympathetically. He put a hand on Williams' shoulder. "Anyway, you're looking for tobacco, and you've come to the right place. How much would you like?"

"An ounce?"

"It's double bubble," Shaun said. "You'll pay two ounces back, okay?"

"No, no, I won't hear of it," Jenner said. "Think of it as a gift to a comrade down on his luck."

Shaun nudged his cellmate. "What are you doing? Everyone will be sponging off you," he hissed.

"Oh, I don't think so," Jenner drawled. He fetched a pouch of tobacco and box of matches. "Do you need skins as well, Tyler?"

"Please. It's either that or use my bible," Williams said.

"Well, we don't want any holy smoke," Jenner said, handing him a packet of papers. "Why don't you light up and tell us more about yourself? Do you need assistance writing letters back home? A special girl, or a special boy, maybe?"

Shaun spluttered into his tea.

Tyler Williams took the bait. "Now you come to mention it, I could use some help writing to Sian. That's my girlfriend. Just to let her know I'm all right. Although," gloom darkened his eyes, "I'd rather be anywhere but here."

As long as it was somewhere he could smoke, Shaun supposed. "She'll think you're in paradise. He can make out that black is white, can our Jens," he said. "Or should I say, Marshall Jenner, MP?"

Williams jumped backwards. "You! With the rent boys?" he asked.

"I'd like to think history will remember me for different reasons," Jenner said. "I voted against the war in Iraq, for example."

"That's enough politics," Shaun said, annoyed that Jenner was taking the moral high ground. "You never asked for more cash for the prison service, when you had the chance."

"True, but I supported cuts in police numbers," Jenner told him. "You see, I look after my friends." He smiled at Tyler Williams. "Rest assured, I don't expect anything from you in return for letter-writing and a bit of tobacco. We're all in this together, eh?" He patted the man's back.

Williams rolled a cigarette and appeared mollified, thanking both of them as he took his leave.

Shaun shook his head. "What was all that about?" he asked.

"I don't expect anything from him," Jenner repeated. "You know I write about a dozen letters a day without requesting payment."

Shaun couldn't argue. Although most inmates gave Jenner tobacco or sugar as a token of gratitude, he didn't demand it. "Are you really giving burn away?" he asked.

"Yes," Jenner replied. "It's obvious the young man's having a miserable time without it. I look after my friends, as I said."

"You just met him," Shaun pointed out.

"Who knows what the future holds?" Jenner said, deadpan.

That was too much information. Shaun finished his tea and paid Jonesy's cell a visit. He found Geoff Jones playing poker with his cellmate, Kevin Kemble. That wouldn't end well. A short, intense man in his early forties, Kemble was the nearest they had to a professional gambler on their wing. He'd made good money selling a system for betting on horse races. Unfortunately, he'd lost all of it and more, causing him to defraud his employer and pay the price with a prison sentence. Nevertheless, unless he was high on the heroin Shaun sold him from a stash in a fellow prisoner's cell, Kemble generally won games of chance against less experienced players on his landing.

"You're on to a loser, Jonesy," Shaun observed, lurking in a corner of the room and watching with amusement as Jones folded after another two rounds.

Jones grinned. "We were just having a bit of fun. Kev can't get a partner any more, can you, Kev?"

"Talking of partners," Shaun said, "since when were you pimping for Jens?"

"Chill," Jones said. "The lad was desperate for a smoke, and I knew Jens could help him out. If he wants to be buggered later, what's the harm?" He cackled.

It was a fair point. Shaun decided to let it go. It wasn't as if the young Welshman was his son. Having done time in Cardiff, Williams should be able to look after himself.

"Wish me luck, Al," Jones said. "I've got a parole hearing tomorrow."

"Of course. Best of British," Shaun said.

Kemble, the little gambler, threw down his cards with a face like thunder. He stormed out.

"What?" Shaun asked.

"He's jealous," Geoff Jones said. "Kev's only a year into his stretch and he's going stir-crazy."

"I guess you don't want to wind him up," Shaun said.

"I'm not scared of him, if that's what you mean," Jones said. "He's got to learn not to be so touchy. I may not get parole anyway. They knocked me back last time."

"Crossing fingers," Shaun said. A rush of nausea filled him as he realised it would be decades before his own chance of parole: long years of boredom, risky business and lonely nights. He had to find a way out soon, before his spirit was crushed to atoms.

Chapter 10.   KAT

Kat met Tim for lunch in a coffee bar. He was sitting inside by the window overlooking St Paul's Church. It was a quiet Tuesday in April, and Kat wasn't required at the casino.

Tim, dashing in a suit, hair freshly cut, stood to greet her. "What can I get you?" he asked, after he'd kissed her cheek. "I'm having the all-day breakfast myself."

"Black coffee, please," Kat said, sliding into the chair opposite.

"Sure that's all?"

On being reassured it was, he went to the counter to order.

Kat looked out of the window at the white stone bulk of St Paul's. There were still jewellers in the area, she knew: rows of small workshops displaying glittering treats in their windows. Still, she couldn't imagine any of them worshipping there; they didn't live near their workplaces any more. Instead, the local residents were yuppies like Erik, popping into the church for music recitals rather than spiritual fulfilment.

Tim returned to his seat. "Penny for your thoughts?"

"My head's spinning with business plans," Kat admitted, unsure the news would hold Tim's attention. Since their first night together, he'd kept their conversation social. "I saw a bank yesterday to ask for a loan. They turned me down." She grimaced.

"Never mind," Tim said. "There are other banks. How much did you apply for?"

"Sixty thousand pounds," Kat said. "I need fifty to buy kit even before I start seeking premises. Production won't be viable unless I scale up."

"You've just made small batches of vodka, so far?" Tim asked.

"Yes," Kat replied, deciding not to tell him that a batch couldn't fill a Smirnoff bottle.

"It does sound like you to need to get the operation on a more commercial footing," Tim said. "I asked a friend about novelty UV-sensitive bottles – he owns a factory that could make them. It wouldn't be expensive but there's a minimum order level."

She stared at him, stunned. "Thanks," she succeeded in saying. "That was nice of you."

Tim grinned. "Don't mention it. Why are you surprised, anyway? I went to see him because I thought it was important to you. You're obviously serious about making vodka, and I want to support you."

Kat was gripped by a sudden elation. "I didn't think you were interested," she said.

"Of course I want to help you," Tim replied. "If you're not at the stage where you have a product to sell, I can't do much, though."

"As soon as I can make it, you could sell it," Kat said.

"I've got the contacts, and I could go out on the road," Tim said. "But I'd have to leave Snow Mountain. There's no way Dad would allow me to push a competitor's brand as well."

"Let's go into partnership," Kat suggested. "I can't pay you a salary, so we'll share the profits instead."

Tim fingered his chin in contemplation. "I'd love to do that, but I haven't got cash to invest. And I bet you need more than sixty k. Maybe a quarter of a million, even. I'm a salesman, not an accountant, but I'm thinking you'll have to pay rent, bottle the vodka and advertise it. Supposing you couldn't get a big enough bank loan, who were you planning to ask? Family and friends?"

"Do I need to remind you my parents are dead?" Kat said. Her cheeks flushed.

"No, you don't, and I'm sorry," Tim said. "I thought…"

"It's just me and my brother," she interrupted, "and Erik's got nothing. He's totally reliant on your father to finance his research. In fact, he's Marty's little puppet." Was it a mistake to get too close to the Bridges family? Her father had lost his life and her brother his independence.

"Wait." Tim's blue eyes fixed hers, his gaze sincere. "Before you jump to conclusions, please remember I'm not my father. Yes, he's heavy-handed and dictatorial. That frustrates me, too. We can work together differently, you and me." He sighed. "I get the picture, though. We need to raise funds for Starshine Vodka. My Dad's got that kind of money, you know." He stopped, clearly noting Kat was on the point of mutiny. "Okay, you're unimpressed by that idea. I'll take a begging bowl to my friends and my bank manager."

"Isn't your flat worth enough?" she asked boldly. Her ex-fiancé's would have been but, as with Marty, she would never swallow her pride to ask him.

"I don't have that level of equity in it," Tim said, without rancour.

Coffee and food was brought to their table. Kat was rarely hungry, and that suited her just fine. Caffeine and cigarettes had always helped her maintain an hourglass figure. She watched her lover tuck into bacon and eggs without feeling the slightest craving.

He finished, and checked his phone. "I had an appointment round the corner after lunch, but it's been cancelled," he said. "I'd really like to see your vodka still. Could we go there now, do you think?"

She couldn't refuse. Naturally, Tim needed proof that she was really making vodka. Otherwise, she could be buying it at a supermarket for all he knew. How would he respond to the tiny scale of her operation, though? And could she be certain he wouldn't tell Marty about it?

"I assume it isn't far, as you asked to meet here," Tim pressed her.

"It's the other side of the church," Kat said. "I'm afraid I built the still on a shoestring. You'll see." She hoped it wouldn't deter him.

"Do you live there too?" he asked.

"Yes, actually. Sure it's just the still you want to see?" she fired back.

"Well, maybe not," Tim acknowledged, chuckling.

"Ready to go?" she asked, excited at the prospect of lingering in the bedroom with him despite her anxiety.

They walked hand in hand through the graveyard, which was criss-crossed with avenues of trees radiating like spokes from the church in the centre. Their destination lay in the heart of the Jewellery Quarter, where media companies and bars sat cheek by jowl with precious metal workshops. After a few minutes, Kat led Tim into Leopold Passage.

To her, even in bright sunlight, the cobbled alleyway was claustrophobic. It was a narrow path with tall terracotta-coloured buildings rising on either side, sheer as cliffs. After a sharp bend, the lane widened into a yard, at the end of which was Marty's property.

Kat wasn't certain he realised the it belonged to his father. The column of buzzers next to the smart black door had neatly typed names next to it, but the shared workspace occupied by Darria Enterprises simply bore the word "office". Tim made no comment as she unlocked the door and ushered him into the lobby.

Her stilettos clattered on the black and white tiled floor. This was an imposing room in its own right, freshly painted in pale blue when Marty refurbished the building. A statement modern chandelier fashioned like a cluster of icicles hung from the second floor through a central void in the polished oak stairwell.

"I remember decorating this hallway," Tim said.

Kat stiffened. That settled her unspoken question: he knew after all.

"When Dad did the building up, he roped us all in," Tim continued. "I gave your brother's flat a lick of paint, too. Is that where you're staying?"

"Yes," Kat admitted.

"Erik's seeing Amy, our marketing manager, isn't he? Why don't we all have a night out together; the four of us?" Tim suggested.

"It's difficult with my shifts," Kat said, not wishing to concede she found Amy spiky.

"How is Erik?" Tim asked.

"Fine. He won't disturb us – he's at work," Kat said.

"In the office?" Tim gestured to his left, at the etched glass door that gave access to the open plan workspace. "Where's the still?"

"Down here," Kat said, indicating a plainer, white glossed door opposite. She opened it, revealing the smell of fermented potato. With the flick of a switch, a light shone on steps leading downwards. She strode to the bottom, Tim following her.

The cellar had once been lined with bricks and earth. Easily the shabbiest room in what was then a down-at-heel, semi-derelict workshop, it had been transformed into a sterile workplace. The walls had been plastered and painted with a white, washable paint, while the floor and stairs were covered in sealed wooden laminate. Scrubbed wood and steel workbenches held Erik's scientific instruments, Kat's demijohns and a sterilisation tank. Proudly, she showed Tim the three stills. "What do you think?" she asked.

Tim's features were inscrutable. "It's all rather Heath Robinson," he managed eventually.

"It's a smaller version of the Snow Mountain distillery," Kat said. She took satisfaction in making a top-quality product with cheap equipment. Nevertheless, his reaction made her hesitate to show him the Smirnoff bottle upstairs.

"I guess you're right," Tim said. He seemed to relax. "Where does the spirit condense? I suppose you've taken the flue liner up to the top floor?"

It was obvious that he wanted to see it. Reluctantly, Kat ushered him to Erik's attic flat.

61

Tim's eyes were drawn, not to the series of vessels in Erik's living room, but the battered red leather sofa that dominated the space. "That was ours," he murmured. "When we were growing up – my brother, my sisters and I. It was in our playroom."

She'd thought it seemed familiar. It was typical of penny-pinching Marty Bridges to foist his old cast-off furniture on Erik, Kat thought sourly.

Filling the silence, Tim pointed to the wall. "That picture over there is Erik's graduation photo, isn't it?"

In a raven's wing gown, beaming under a black mortar board, a younger Erik was standing next to his parents and eleven-year-old Kat. Youthful and good looking, frozen in time, Alexander and Maria Belov smiled at the camera.

Kat nodded. It was the single picture of their parents that she and Erik possessed. "That was taken in England, up North," she said. "Erik graduated from Manchester. I wish my parents had never gone back to Bazakistan afterwards. Three years later, the police came for my father." She drew a finger across her throat.

"It's a police state," Tim said. "We're lucky it's different here."

"Do you really believe that?" Kat asked. "I tell you, if I see so much as a traffic warden's uniform, I run the other way."

"You don't even drive!" Tim said. As she frowned, the laughter died on his lips. He squeezed her hand. "You know, you look so like your mother, it's uncanny. And Erik resembles your father. Sasha Belov. I met him a couple of times. He was extraordinarily kind. He badgered Dad to let me stay on at school."

Kat blinked away tears. "Only family and close friends called my father Sasha," she said.

"Dad thought of him as family," Tim replied. "He said they were like brothers."

Kat trembled with a toxic mixture of anguish and pain. "No brother would…" she began to say.

Tim put a finger to her lips. "Hush. I'm sorry. Again." He enveloped her in a hug, stroking her hair, kissing her lightly.

A heady pull of desire for him overwhelmed her once more. Kat didn't resist when Tim locked the apartment door and pulled her down onto the big red sofa.

Chapter 11.   JERRY

Jerry Shanahan looked out of his living room window, set in an oblong, pebbledashed bay identical to all the others in this long, straight suburban street in Ilford. He cursed as he lit his cigarette. The Jobcentre had summoned him to discuss his disability benefit that afternoon. There was business to be done first, and his friend was late.

Finally, Scott arrived, parking his sporty red Mazda MX-5 on the patterned brick drive. As Jerry watched, the smaller man emerged from his car, strutted to the front door and rang the bell.

"We got time for a cuppa char?" Scott asked.

Jerry looked at his watch. "Just," he said.

Scott swaggered into the living room and sprawled on the sofa. Jerry stubbed out his cigarette and made drinks: instant coffee for himself and PG Tips for his friend. There was no need to ask Scott how he took it: away from the girlfriend, it involved full fat milk and three sugars.

While both were in their late forties, sporting beerguts and muscled limbs decorated with tattoos, they appeared an ill-matched pair. Jerry was tall and gregarious, while Scott was short and reserved. That wasn't the only difference. Although nominally resident in Essex, Jerry was a Londoner in spirit. Anyone passing through the urban sprawl of Ilford would consider it part of the neighbouring city. In contrast, Scott had decamped to the countryside, to his lover's ancient cottage by the River Lee in Broxbourne. The girlfriend was a vegetarian who did yoga; she wanted Scott to adopt her toxin-free, smoothie-drinking, middle class lifestyle. Jerry had no truck with it; he smoked for Britain, to Scott's disgust. Nonetheless, they were an efficient team, having worked together for several years. Their common interest in West Ham, strong beer and making a dishonest living was enough.

"Where do you want to go?" Scott asked, slurping his tea.

"The Forest Road," Jerry said. They were planning a run to Bruges again. It was advisable to take orders in advance, not least because some of their sales were made to pubs, and landlords were picky. Jerry reckoned he'd be the same; there was no point stocking Stella if your customers wanted the stronger stuff.

"Best of a bad job, I suppose," Scott said. "It was easier when Shaun was around. That Jon is as much use as a chocolate teapot."

"Give the lad a chance," Jerry said, although he was beginning to share Scott's reservations. There were other gangs encroaching on their turf. Young Jon wasn't respected and feared enough to provide the protection his father had given.

"It's not like the old days in the East End," Scott said.

Jerry agreed. Hawking bootlegged booze in the backstreets of Walthamstow wasn't as easy as it used to be. Yuppies had moved into the Stow; they weren't interested in buying from him and he didn't trust them anyway. While his traditional customer base still frequented the area, there were fewer places to reach them. There was CCTV in most of the carparks where he used to sell his wares, outside pubs, clubs and leisure centres. Still, some camera-free outlets remained. He favoured a couple of pubs with accommodating landlords, men who turned a blind eye to outdoor sales in exchange for a wad of notes.

They left the Mazda on the drive and took Jerry's white Transit from his lock-up around the corner. Their first stop was a bar that had recently changed hands. Previously a typical local with dark brown furniture and sticky carpets, it had been bought by a chain and closed for refurbishment.

"Look, it's open again," Jerry said, pulling into the carpark. There were lights in the windows, two clipped conical bushes in pots on either side of the door, and a freestanding blackboard offering fine food and craft beers.

"Any cameras?" Scott asked.

They both peered at the corners of the building. Jerry saw nothing except a couple of large metal chains around the potted bushes. That would protect the containers, he supposed.

There was a new name on the sign above the door. Neither of them could read it.

"What do you think that says?" Jerry asked.

"Foreign innit?" Scott said, with a shrug. "Let's forget it. Why take risks? We don't know him."

"Paul used to buy ten crates at a time," Jerry said. Without letting Scott reply, he pushed the door open.

Inside, fresh-faced staff had arrived along with the pastel paint and stripped wooden floors. Jerry asked a girl for the manager.

"Bobby? He's changing the beer over," she said, in an accent that was a curious mixture of East End and Eastern Europe.

"Who wants me?" The brisk young man emerged behind the bar from a plain pine door.

"That your name outside?" Jerry asked.

"Yes," Bobby replied. "Don't tell me: it's impossible to pronounce. That's why they call me Bobby. How can I help?" He was tall, thin and swarthy, his expression one of polite interest. It was evident English wasn't his first language, but he spoke it well.

Jerry grinned. "Paul, who had your job before, told me to see you," he lied. He guessed Bobby's predecessor was long gone; anyhow, even if the two men spoke to each other, Paul would put in a good word. "Where are you from, by the way?"

"I was managing a pub in Bedford," Bobby said. "Before that, Romania. Why did Paul send you?"

"I used to bring him a lot of lager. Spirits as well, at low prices," Jerry said.

"Basically," Scott said, "anything you want, we'll get it for you. And for your mates."

Suspicion settled into Bobby's features. "It isn't stolen, is it?" he asked, in a less friendly tone.

"Not at all," Jerry said. "I pick it up in Bruges. Like he says, the choice is yours. You name it, I'll fetch it for you."

Bobby glanced to either side. "Nina, can you collect glasses, please," he commanded the girl. Waiting until she was out of earshot, he said, "I'm interested. Everyone likes a bargain, after all. But I don't want any of that dirt-cheap lager Paul had from you." He pointed to a row of optics. "See, the new owners are after an affluent clientele. High-end spirits and Trappist beers. What sort of prices are we talking about anyway? It has to be worth my while."

Jerry negotiated mutually satisfactory volumes and rates, and agreed to return on Saturday.

"Bring extra for my friends," Bobby said, beaming. "I'll ask a few of them over. We'll give you a warm welcome."

As he returned to the van, Jerry wondered why the manager's smile hadn't reached his eyes.

Chapter 12.   MARTY

Marty Bridges' warehouse was located in a street which, although half a mile from both Birmingham city centre and the canalside bars of Brindleyplace, had so far resisted attempts at gentrification. Here, East West Bridges Ltd stored its flagship Snow Mountain vodka, darria teabags, and anything else on which Marty could turn a profit.

A 1970s extension fronting onto the road housed a suite of offices. Of these, only one had any size or elegance. A nameplate on its heavy oak door announced "Mr Bridges". Behind it, the room was both panelled and furnished in bird's eye maple. Elsewhere, a corridor led to small, partitioned spaces, which Amy and other East West Bridges staff beautified as best they could with posters and plants.

Marty could have chosen to meet Angela's tennis club friend at his workplace. However, when she'd suggested afternoon tea at a trendy bar, he'd agreed at once. He was packing a few samples of vodka and darria when the oak door swung open.

"Have you got a minute, Dad?" Tim asked, hovering at the threshold.

Marty clocked the excited, nervous edge to his eldest son's voice, then looked at his watch. "I can give you ten," he said.

"Great." Tim perched on a black leather visitor's chair, his elbows on Marty's desk. "Dad, I've been asked to work with a craft vodka brand, Starshine. In fact, I'm going to be a partner in the business."

"Never heard of them," Marty interjected. He wasn't convinced he needed another vodka in his portfolio either. "I thought you were in London today, seeing Fortnum & Mason."

"I'm meeting their buyer tomorrow," Tim said. "Listen, Dad. Starshine is like a smaller version of Snow Mountain. The vodka is smooth, creamy and distinctive. I think it will really go places. But the team needs investment. We're looking at two hundred and fifty grand to buy plant, premises, get a licence to sell alcohol and so on."

That explained the nerves. Tim wanted money. "I'll need to see a business plan," Marty said. "Also, you mentioned a licence. Don't you have one already?"

Tim's brow furrowed. "We're not selling the product yet," he said.

"You need one to distil alcohol as well as sell it," Marty pointed out. Distilling was a dangerous business. It produced alcohol so concentrated that it would ignite with a single spark. It wasn't just the vodka makers who needed to beware; any methanol in the spirit, and customers would go blind.

"I'm sure we've got a licence then. I'll check," Tim said. "You can be sure I'll apply for one if it's been overlooked." There wasn't a tremor in his voice, but he was clearly wrong-footed.

"You do that," Marty said, glancing at his watch again. "Got to go. When can I meet the Starshine Vodka team?"

Tim looked shifty. "We're not at that stage yet," he said. "No one knows I'm talking to you."

"You've got work to do, then," Marty said. "Forgive me, but I like to know who I'm doing business with." He kept a poker face despite his relief that one of his children was displaying an entrepreneurial spark at last. "Keep me posted," he added, standing up and walking to the door so that Tim was obliged to leave.

The appointment was in ten minutes' time. Marty decided to walk; the bar was on the way to the station, in an old sorting office that had been transformed into upmarket shops and eateries.

Angela and her friend were waiting for him side by side on a plush banquette. He noticed they were wearing similar styles: tight jeans and strappy tops that accentuated their tanned skin and slim figures. Two empty champagne flutes rested on the round wooden table in front of them.

"You didn't expect me to be early, did you?" Angela said, laughing.

"I didn't think you'd start on champagne at this time of day, either," Marty said, his mind flicking back to his lunch with Harry two months before.

"It's Prosecco," Angela's companion said. "Want another, Angela?"

"Oh, yes," Angela giggled, "and one for Marty."

"That would be me," Marty said, extending his right hand.

"I'm Joanne." Her voice was plummier than Angela's, and indeed Marty's own, Midlands twang. She rose, air-kissing his cheek and applying the lightest of pressures to his hand. It was like being introduced to a ghost.

As thin and short as Angela, Joanne was about twenty years younger, with short, wavy black hair and a pointed face. Her brown eyes were lined with sparkly lilac and boasted feathery, obviously false, black eyelashes.

"Joanne's really interested in darria," Angela said.

"You're a journalist, I understand," Marty enquired.

Joanne simpered. "I'm mainly known for my wellness blog," she said, "but I write for The Huffington Post as well." She took an iPhone from a capacious, squashy sky-blue handbag and patted the seat beside her. "Sit down, Marty, and we'll do a little video for my website."

He did as he was told. Joanne thrust her face right next to his, tapping the phone's screen and angling it towards them.

"I'm here in Birmingham," Joanne said, "with Martyn Bridges, a local entrepreneur who's beginning a skincare revolution. Read all about it in my blog." She jabbed at the phone again and placed it on the table, moving sideways to give Marty his personal space back.

"You're recording me?" he said.

Joanne shrugged. "Why not?"

A waiter was hovering. Angela smiled at him. "Three afternoon teas, a bottle of Prosecco and another glass, please," she said.

"So," Joanne said, "tell me about darria, the miracle anti-ageing herb."

"I first visited Bazakistan for my vodka business," Marty said. "I import Snow Mountain, a high-end brand."

"That's good stuff," Joanne said, evidently impressed.

"You like it, Joanne?" Angela asked. "We should have ordered cocktails."

"Are you driving?" Marty asked his wife.

"Carry on," Joanne commanded.

Marty returned his attention to her. "Darria is a shrub that grows wild in Bazakistan," he said. "It can be made into a tea that's quite pleasant to drink." He was stretching a point here; he couldn't stand the taste himself. "Anyway, it's especially popular in the mountain valleys to the southwest of the city of Kireniat. My business partner, Erik White, comes from the area. He noticed that villagers in the valleys lived for an incredibly long time. Centenarians aren't unusual. He synthesised the active ingredient from darria and discovered it cured cancer."

"Hold on," Angela said. "I thought you weren't allowed to say that about darria, Marty?"

"Thanks, Angela. Sorry, the reference to cancer is off the record, Joanne," Marty said hastily.

"What a shame." Joanne's disappointment was palpable, although fortunately eased by the arrival of Prosecco and a chrome cake stand containing miniature sandwiches and sweet treats.

"They're a bit small," Marty observed.

"That's right," Angela said. "You don't need to lay down more timber. A little of what you fancy…"

"Or a lot, in the case of Prosecco," Marty said, splashing the fizz into three glasses. The waiter brought a teapot, milk jug and cups, which remained untouched.

"Tell me about Erik White," Joanne said. "That doesn't sound like a foreign name. There must be a story there."

"He's naturalised British," Angela said. "He changed his name, didn't he, Marty?"

"Yes. He was born Erik Belov. That means 'White' in Russian," Marty said.

"He's a handsome young fellow," Angela said. "But don't go getting ideas, Jo. He's spoken for."

"As am I," Joanne said smoothly. "I'm married to Bob Beale, Marty. I think you know him?"

"Indeed," Marty agreed. A fellow freemason, Bob headed one of the largest manufacturing conglomerates in the Midlands. Joanne must be his third wife; they were younger every time.

Joanne switched back to interview mode. "When did you and Erik begin working together?"

"Two years ago," Marty said. "We set up a joint venture to fund Erik's cancer research by selling darria tea as a food supplement. It's reputed to have anti-ageing properties…"

"You use it, don't you, Angela?" Joanne interrupted. "What do you think of it?"

"It's given my skin a new lease of life," Angela said.

"She looks great on it, doesn't she?" Marty said fondly.

"Haven't you had other work done?" Joanne asked her. "Threading, for example?"

Marty wondered why the discussion had turned to sewing. "What Angela does in her spare time is none of my business," he said.

Joanne gave him a sharp look. "I'll take a few pictures of you, Angela, if you don't mind."

Marty helped himself to tiny scones and muffins while Angela posed prettily for Joanne's iPhone. He checked his emails, seeing to his irritation that a purchase of farmland had just fallen through.

"What are your plans for darria?" Joanne asked when the impromptu photo shoot had ended. "As a skin treatment, I mean."

"I want to scale up production," Marty said, his mouth full of cake. "More women deserve to treat themselves to darria. It's affordable pampering." He was on-message with his marketing-speak, he told himself.

"How exactly do you grow darria?" Joanne asked.

"On an allot…," Angela said.

Marty kicked her ankle. He needed a better source of darria than Erik's friend's allotment, but he couldn't afford to let The Huffington Post know his raw materials were in short supply. Anyway, there was plenty of agricultural land near Birmingham and he would soon find another farm to buy. "Believe it or not," he began, racking his brain for an end to the sentence and thankfully finding one, "darria isn't the only plant that grows like a weed in Bazakistan. Cannabis does too. So I guess I need to find a marijuana farmer to cultivate darria for me."

Joanne perked up. "Can I quote you on that?" she asked.

"Why not?" Marty said. It would attract attention to the product. Surely no publicity was bad publicity?

Chapter 13.   SHAUN

"Who's kicking off?" Shaun grumbled. He'd been waiting in the dinner queue for five minutes, and he was hungry. At the head of the line, another prisoner was berating the server, threatening violence if a larger portion wasn't forthcoming.

"New boy," Geoff Jones said. "Lifer. Just been sent down for murder."

"I'll murder him in a minute," Shaun said. "He's got no right to throw his weight about. Why aren't the screws stopping him?"

The answer was obvious: at almost seven feet tall, the new inmate loomed menacingly over the servery.

"Never mind the jolly giant," Jones said, as half a dozen prison officers arrived to restore order, "I've got news. Come and see me later."

Shaun almost forgot in his haste to obtain and eat his supper. There was a mere half hour of the evening association period remaining when he recalled the conversation with the jewel thief.

"Where's Kemble?" Shaun asked, surprised Jones was alone in his cell.

"Playing cards with Jolly," Jones said.

The nickname was evidently going to stick. Shaun grinned. Kemble hadn't wasted any time finding a new victim to bleed. "He'd better be careful then. Think Jolly will be a good loser?"

"I've got parole, Al," Jones whispered. "Out tomorrow after breakfast."

"Well done, mate." Shaun was pleased for him. They'd known each other, inside and out, for years. He understood why Jonesy didn't want his good fortune to be common knowledge, with Kemble being so sensitive.

"You know how it is, Al. Tell a soul, and all the cons descend like vultures, scrounging your stuff. I'll take the burn with me, but I'll leave the biscuits and tuna for Kev. To make it a bit easier for him, you know."

Like most of the lags, Jones had bought a few luxuries with money he'd earned in the prison workshop. Shaun suspected Kemble would barter the goods for tobacco. He kept his misgivings to himself.

"I'd like you to have something, though, Al. To remember me by. And it might be useful." Proudly, Jones removed a trainer and peeled the insole upwards. Below it lay a shiv, a home-made knife fashioned from a plastic toothbrush. The end had been melted and two razor blades inserted parallel to each other. Maybe three millimetres apart, they were designed to scar. When the shiv was used, it would create a wound that couldn't be stitched.

Shaun stared at it. "How come you didn't set off the metal detectors?" he asked.

Geoff Jones smirked. "I've got a bionic leg, remember?" He pulled the hem of his left trouser leg upwards, revealing a lattice of white scar tissue. "Motorbike accident. There are pins in it, and I've got a certificate. All the screws know."

"Impressive, but I can hardly pull the same stunt," Shaun said. "I tell you what, leave it with Bartlett. He needs it to protect my gear."

Nobody risked being caught with drugs when they could find someone else prepared to store them at a price. If young Adam Bartlett's cell was searched by the authorities, it wouldn't be just the shiv they'd find.

"Let me know if you change your mind," Jones said.

"Thanks, mate, I appreciate the offer but it's too tricky with only twenty minutes to bang-up," Shaun said. "All the best, though." He shook his friend's hand before returning to his cell. Maybe Jens would have a cup of tea ready for him.

He wasn't prepared for the sight of the jolly giant almost filling the room, his back to the door and his arms pounding vigorously.

"What are you doing in my pad?" Shaun yelled. Almost instantly, he realised Jenner was in the corner, obscured from view and the target of the volatile giant's ire.

He had to act quickly. Jenner might have stood a chance against a man his own size, but he was no match for Jolly. Shaun picked up his kettle, the heaviest object to hand, and brought it down hard on the giant's head.

With a roar, Jolly turned around, fists flailing in front of him. Shaun fought dirty. It was second nature. He stamped on Jolly's feet, clad in flimsy tennis shoes, before springing up to nut the giant.

Jolly howled, but he wasn't beaten. He grabbed Shaun in a bear hug, and squeezed.

Shaun felt himself choking. Desperately, he kicked Jolly's shins. He should have known better than to tackle a psychopath, but what choice did he have? Everyone knew Shaun Halloran didn't run away from a fight. He wasn't going to lose face lightly. Anyway, good cellmates protected each other's backs.

All breath crushed from his lungs, Shaun couldn't even scream as Jolly's knee sent an explosion of pain into his groin. At any moment, his ribs would crack. He prayed Jenner would call for help; he might escape with his life, if not his reputation.

"You want some?" As Shaun gasped for air, blood pounding through his head, he heard Geoff Jones' cold voice.

"I've got a shiv," Jones hissed. "You want some, or what?"

Jones must have given Jolly a flash of the blade, for the big man began to relax his grip. Shaun elbowed his way to freedom, delivering a jab to the giant's groin in the process.

The noise had finally attracted the attention of two screws. Fortunately, one of them was Ed Rothery.

"What's going on?" the other officer said. "Jones, Watson – you know another fella's cell is off limits."

It was the first time Shaun had heard Jolly's name. Jonesy was almost certainly in the same boat, but he lied manfully.

"Sorry, Gov," Geoff Jones said. "Mr Watson here tripped over and we were giving him first aid. Didn't want to bother you, seeing as you're a busy man." This was perilously close to extracting the urine; Shaun was sure all the officers did during association was drink tea and push paperwork around in their office, the glass bubble at the end of the landing.

Watson, his justifiable fear of punishment overcoming animosity, nodded his bloodied head. "That's right," he said.

"All right, I'll let it go," Ed Rothery said. "You should have told us first; that's why Mr, er, Watson's got a call button in his cell."

"He fell on the landing," Jones pointed out.

"And what about him?" the other screw said, pointing to Jenner.

The politician hadn't escaped unscathed. His eyes and lips red and swollen, he said, "I ran into a door."

"Carelessness seems to be contagious," his inquisitor observed.

Rothery rolled his eyes. "For heaven's sake, Tony, leave it. Jones is out on parole tomorrow; then he's the probation service's problem, not ours."

"I suppose you're right," his colleague conceded, with bad grace. "Hurry back to your cell, Jones. And you, Watson."

"May I have a plaster?" the giant whined.

"No you may not. You've given us enough grief already," Tony answered, predictably unsympathetic.

Rothery lingered in the doorway when the other visitors had left. "Try to keep some order in here, Halloran," he said.

Shaun chose his words carefully. Ed might be in his pocket, but he didn't want Jenner to know. "That Mr Watson is trouble, Mr Rothery," he said. "I'd get him off the wing if I were you."

"You could be right," Rothery said, clearly appreciating he'd been given a command. "I'll see what I can do. Time to lock up now, lads."

"It's ten to," Shaun protested. "We'll be banged up long enough tonight. Can't you come back in a few minutes, Gov?"

Rothery made a show of looking at his watch. "Very well. Five minutes. I'll make sure Mr Watson has no more unfortunate accidents on the way to his cell. And," he glared at Jenner, "that no one else does."

"Thanks," Jenner said, once Rothery was out of earshot.

"Don't mention it," Shaun said, relieved that Jens hadn't spoken out of turn. His padmate was becoming one of the lads.

"I assure you, Al, it's a mystery to me why…"

Shaun cut him short. "Why the jolly giant hit you? Maybe because he's a Labour voter, but definitely because he's a psychopath. And he's stupid with it. I'd have slashed him and asked questions afterwards. Jonesy was right not to, though. Why jeopardise his parole?" He made for the door. "Anyway, I need to thank him properly."

He found Geoff Jones back in his cell, making tea. His cellmate, the gambler Kevin Kemble, was doing a Sudoku puzzle, no doubt to keep his mathematical skills honed.

Shaun checked there was no one else around, then stood in the doorway.

"Thanks," he said.

"Don't mention it," Jones replied.

"Thought he was playing cards?" Shaun said, with a glance at Kemble. The gambler didn't look up.

"He won all Jolly's burn off him," Jones said. "Guess he suggested going to Jenner for more. Shame he didn't mention about asking nicely."

"Do you still have the shiv?"

Kemble pricked up his ears.

"Never you mind," Shaun warned the gambler. "Get out of here before I use it on you. You've caused me enough trouble."

Kemble left sulkily, Shaun's glare following him.

"Give me your shoe, then," Jones said. "I couldn't find you know who earlier."

"I guessed," Shaun said. "I'll make sure he has it tomorrow – can't let a finely-honed specimen go to waste." Now it had saved him from the uncontrollable giant, he regarded the home-made knife as a good luck charm.

Shaun watched him transfer the shiv, an operation that took no more than ten seconds. He was grateful that Jones hadn't mentioned Bartlett by name. There was something about Kemble he disliked, for all that the gambler paid for his heroin on time. At least, he assumed Kemble's girlfriend was up to date in the payments she made to Jon. Shaun made a mental note to ask his son.

"Sorted," Geoff Jones said.

"Thanks," Shaun repeated. "You've scratched my back, so I'll scratch yours," he told Jones. It was no fun being released from prison with a mere forty-eight pounds in your pocket. He'd help Geoff earn some serious money, and Geoff could help him too. "See my lad when you're out."

"Your eldest?" Jones asked.

"No, he's hopeless." Shaun had to face facts: they'd never make a villain out of Ben. "The younger one. I'll make sure he knows. When I was caught, I stumbled across tunnels below the Jewellery Quarter in Birmingham."

Jones looked puzzled. "So?"

"It's like Hatton Garden," Shaun said. "I know a way in. I'll tell Jon, and he can tell you. He'll give you money for tools as well. Fifty fifty, all right?"

Jones grinned. "It's great to be back in business."

"Good for both of us," Shaun said. He clapped the wiry thief on the back. "See you around."

Having taken his leave, he wasn't best pleased to see both Kevin Kemble and Tyler Williams loitering on the landing outside. How much had they heard? He hoped it didn't matter. "What do you want?" Shaun snapped.

"Got to be back for bang-up," Kemble muttered. His hooded brown eyes revealed no emotion.

"I told you, any trouble and you'll be sorry," Shaun said, "and that applies to you and all, Boyo."

Williams didn't seem rattled either. "I thought Jonesy might have some burn to spare. He's out tomorrow, you know."

Shaun looked up at the ceiling. News travelled fast. "You can ask him," he said, expecting Jonesy to send the Welshman away with a flea in his ear. Just for once, he was almost looking forward to the sanctuary of his cell.

That feeling dissipated once his door was locked. Jenner didn't offer tea. The MP was subdued. He'd splashed cold water on his face and established no bones or teeth were broken. Now he was silent, writing letters to fulfil a list of requests from other inmates.

Shaun gazed at the images on the wall. Torn from newspapers and magazines, they'd been accompanied by stories of Kat's kidnap by terrorists in Bazakistan a year ago. She also knew, then, what it was like to rot in captivity. Shaun wished she'd stayed there, her life fading away in a cell year after year, as his was. Methodically, he took each picture down, occasionally stroking Kat's face before reattaching the faded paper to the wall with fresh toothpaste.

When he'd last seen her, it had been in the strange, Tube-like tunnels below Birmingham's Jewellery Quarter. The building that had given him access, via a long shaft bored from its cellar, had been virtually derelict. Geoff Jones would have no trouble breaking in. His only problem would be identifying a likely prospect to rob from the many jewellery workshops above ground. Burrowing in through the tunnels should be easy. Shaun hadn't spotted any CCTV cameras in them. It was sheer bad luck that had led to his capture there; that, and stupid Jeb dropping his gun where Kat could pick it up. Jonesy was bound to secure substantial spoils. The jewel thief, already meticulous in his organisation, had spoken highly of the Thinking Skills courses offered within the prison. They'd helped him improve his approach to planning a job, he said.

Kevin Kemble's jealousy was understandable. Shaun, too, longed to be on the outside. Jon had promised to find a way, as soon as he could give his father money in his pocket, a false passport and a sunny bolthole.

That wasn't all Shaun wanted. He stared into paper Kat's green eyes, remembering the hatred in the real thing as she'd stood over him with a gun in her hand. Freedom would mean nothing if he couldn't see those eyes again and fill them with fear.

"Lend us your notepad, Jens," he demanded.

Jenner raised an eyebrow and tore off a sheet for him.

Laboriously scribbling with a pencil in his left hand, Shaun wrote: You're going to die, slut, once I've had my fun.

He stared, satisfied, at his handiwork, wishing he had Kat's address. He'd offered Rothery fifty pounds for it, but while the officer's beady eyes showed he wanted the cash, he'd failed to find out where she lived.

After what seemed like hours, Shaun struck a match and set light to the letter, holding a corner as it blackened and curled. At the last minute, his fingers tingling as the flames reached them, he dropped the smouldering remains.

Jenner didn't even look up. He continued to write, saying nothing about the mess on the floor or the acrid smell. When he finally spoke, it was simply to say, "I'm putting the TV on. It's time for the news."

Shaun nodded his permission. As the television blared into life, the talking heads and disasters of the day filled his consciousness like white noise, and his desires slipped back into the darkest corners of his mind.

Chapter 14.   ERIK

Kat popped her head through the door of the open-plan office. "I'm going to work," she told Erik.

"You'll be busy, I guess," he said.

His sister shrugged. "I don't know. Richie said the first May bank holiday weekend was quiet last year. I've got some extra shifts, though, so they must be expecting tourists as well as the regulars."

"I hope your gamblers are in a holiday mood and generous with their tips," he said, as she closed the door. Perhaps, with an increase in hours at the casino and more money, she'd move out.

"Who was that?" Geoff Smith was the only other person left in the office on Friday afternoon. An IT consultant, older than Erik by at least twenty years, he'd just begun renting a desk there.

"My sister," Erik said. He was surprised to hear from Geoff. Quiet and unassuming, the older man avoided small talk.

"She looked familiar," Geoff said. "I must have confused her with someone else." He lowered his eyes and began to type on his laptop, signalling an end to the conversation.

It had been a long week. Erik still had work to do, but he wanted a break. "I'm going to call it a day," he said, putting his MacBook into the black rubber messenger bag Amy had bought him for Christmas. "How about you, Geoff? Leaving soon?"

Geoff didn't look up. "No mate. Got a deadline to meet on my project," he said, in a Cockney accent so broad that even Erik, a foreigner, could recognise it.

"Are you going home to London this weekend?" Erik asked.

"As long as I get this finished," Geoff said. "I'll have to stay over if I don't." He looked at his watch. "Last train's not till eleven."

Geoff had no luggage with him, Erik noticed. The computer expert couldn't be expecting to catch the train. A wave of sympathy compelled him to stop by the door. "I hope you get back today," he said. "It's a bank holiday, after all."

"Don't worry about me," Geoff said. "Do you have any plans yourself?"

"I'm going away with my girlfriend," Erik said.

"Dirty weekend, eh?" Geoff cackled. "Don't let me keep you."

Erik was too tired to correct him. Amy was dragging him to London to stay with her father, so a sex-crazed mini-break was hardly in prospect. He flashed a feeble smile at Geoff before returning to Amy's studio on the top floor.

Amy was right to complain. It was too small for them both, and the cramped conditions were placing a strain on their relationship. He resolved to talk to his sister the following week. He would sit down with Kat, help her calculate a budget for rent, food and utilities. If necessary, he would subsidise her.

Erik's own needs were modest. For years, he had scrimped and saved to fund his cancer research, living on a shoestring. The habit remained despite the regular income he was now drawing from the business. If Kat would move to a less desirable area, he could spare enough cash for her to lease a two bedroomed flat. She'd need plenty of space to accommodate her distillery. Again, Amy's concerns were justified. Kat had been nothing but trouble to Marty; he'd see the still in the cellar as a betrayal. That wouldn't just cause problems for Erik. He was Marty's business partner, but Amy was an employee.

He was still mulling over his options when she returned from work.

"You left the light on in the office," she said.

"That'll be Geoff," Erik said. "He's still working there."

"Geoff?"

"He's an IT consultant working on a project in Birmingham," Erik said. "Disaster recovery for an office that burned down. Obviously, they haven't got a desk for him."

"The go-to guy for your IT problems, then?"

"Not exactly." Apart from telling them to switch the machines off and on again, the Londoner's knowledge didn't extend to fixing problems with the Macs that everyone else in the office used. As far as Erik could deduce from occasional glimpses of Geoff's screen, the work involved reading maps, drawing pictures and watching porn.

"Anyway," Amy said, "you didn't tell me you were working with dope farmers to grow darria."

"Marty's little joke," Erik said.

"Really? Marty sounded serious about it in his interview with The Huffington Post," Amy said.

"What?" Erik didn't read The Huffington Post and was unaware that Marty had even heard of it.

"He said he'd like to meet marijuana farmers," Amy said.

Erik groaned. "I'll put him right." He removed his phone from his pocket. Marty's was the last number he'd dialled. Erik tapped it again.

The call went straight to voicemail. "Marty, we don't need to sully our mission by working with drugs traders. Can you give me a call about the latest on darria in The Huffington Post, please," Erik said into the ether, before snapping his phone shut. "I need a drink, Amy. How about a night out at the tavern?"

"Dinner with cocktails? You're on."

Geoff was locking the office as they left the property. He hadn't finished, he explained; he would work the next morning. Feeling sorry for him, Erik was about to ask the IT consultant to join them at the Rose Villa Tavern when Geoff yawned, declaring he was exhausted. He'd be returning to his hotel for in-room movies and an early night.

Evenings were becoming longer again. Sunbeams danced in the courtyard outside the converted jewellery workshop, causing the high brick walls to glow bright red. Even the dull cobbles underfoot took on flashes of colour: chocolate, lilac, green. Unlike the forests and fields of his homeland, this city had a subtle beauty, often revealed in fleeting moments such as this. Erik squeezed Amy's hand.

Until his parents died, he hadn't anticipated making a home in England. Nor, once he'd done so, had Erik expected a long-term relationship. He'd thrown himself into research; anything to forget the reality of being an orphan, of having no future in Bazakistan. That focus on work had made him self-contained, slipping into casual liaisons when women pursued him, but otherwise ignoring them. His passion for Amy was a new and intoxicating sensation.

Tonight, she was radiating happiness. He hoped she would never know the bitter pain of seeing loved ones' lives brutally cut short. Unable to save his parents, Erik had vowed he'd do anything to protect his sister from harm. Now he saw that he felt the same way about Amy.

Amy, auburn hair vivid in the last rays of sun, smiled at him without an inkling of his dark thoughts. "I should try a few different vodkas tonight," she said. "Purely in the interests of research. To compare them with Snow Mountain. And just maybe because it's Bank Holiday Friday. A few days off are exactly what I need."

Erik felt guilty that he hadn't asked about her work. "Oh?" he prompted.

"Yes. Harry Aliyev is being a nuisance. Now we've met, he's taken to ringing me up, supposedly to talk about his product. In a heavy-handed way, he then says he feels he should visit Paris on business, can I recommend a hotel, and would I care to join him? I complained to Marty, but he laughed and said all I have to do is say no."

"And did you?"

"Repeatedly. You shouldn't need to ask." Amy frowned.

The vodka maker was old enough to be her grandfather. Erik felt his hatred of Aliyev increasing, although he wouldn't previously have believed it possible. "Don't tell me when he's in Birmingham again. I won't be responsible for my actions," he said.

"Don't worry," Amy said. "I can handle the old sleazebag. If Marty can make a joke out of it, so can I. I need a drink, though, and Kat recommends a cherrytini."

The vibrantly-hued cocktails served at the pub were a mystery to Erik. He duly ordered one on their arrival, accompanying it with the dark beer he preferred. Marty, who had tutored him towards real ales, was fond of saying he'd sell vodka to those who liked it but he had better taste himself.

Amy showed him the Huffington Post article while they waited for their food. It was a short piece, focusing on the soft launch of the anti-ageing tea. There was a photograph of Angela smiling winsomely next to Marty. Below it, she was quoted as a satisfied consumer of the product.

"Great publicity for darria," she said.

"It is," Erik conceded. He was relieved that the feature was carefully worded, merely hinting at darria's rejuvenating properties and making no mention of its cancer-busting potential. That, of course, was the primary focus of his research, but the law prevented him from publicising it before the drug was proven to work. Meanwhile, clinical trials were costly, so much so that Darria Enterprises could afford them only by marketing overpriced teabags to women of advancing years. "I'm a bit put out, actually," he added. "Marty didn't mention this at all." He had to raise it with his business partner.

Erik relaxed as the beer took effect, especially after a second pint and a third. They discussed their impending visit to London. "I'll need to go to the allotment first, and probably the office as well," Erik said. Geoff wasn't the only one with unfinished work.

Amy said she'd hoped for an early start, but the next morning, she was still half-asleep when Erik left her flat. Having noted her bleary eyes and desultory wave of farewell, he imagined she'd doze until midday.

He set off on his bicycle, a battered old workhorse kept in the courtyard outside. As Leopold Passage was a narrow, twisting alley, there were few passers-by; had any been light-fingered, there were more tempting prospects elsewhere. His ride to the allotments took fifteen minutes, most of it spent on canal towpaths. During the week, he might have seen a few commuters and joggers, but he met no one at 7.30am on a Saturday.

The allotment was on the way to the university, not far from Marty's home. Erik unlocked the access gate and pushed his bike across a rough track to the patch where he tended several rows of darria shrubs. There were thirty two in all, neatly laid out in lines. Between them, his friend grew root vegetables and herbs.

Erik removed tools from the tiny shed next to the patch: shears, hoe, fork and spade. As with his bicycle, they were sturdy, ancient and unattractive to thieves. The shed was never locked. His first task was to weed the plot, the price he paid for his unofficial use of the land. Dandelions and rosebay willowherb, self-seeded in the autumn, were thrusting through the soil. There was also a plant, its name unknown to him, that would produce a little blue flower; it spread persistently through its root system and was therefore difficult to remove without destroying the young carrots too. He hoed the aggressor as best he could.

After a mild winter, his darria was beginning to produce buds already. Erik clipped them to promote leaf growth. Tenderly, he scooped spadefuls of compost from a conical bin, mulching the base of each shrub. At last, content with his efforts, he cleaned the tools and replaced them in the shed. The entire process had taken two hours.

He'd always adored gardening. As he cycled back, Erik recalled the grounds around his parents' bungalow in Kireniat: being dwarfed by majestic foxgloves as a tiny boy, scattering marigold seeds when he was slightly older, and finally being trusted to cultivate strawberries. The memory of their sweetness lingered on his lips.

Back in the Jewellery Quarter at ten, he unlocked Amy's door as quietly as he could, tiptoeing to the shower room. He needed a wash and a change of clothes after his exertions on the land. Refreshed, he checked she was still asleep before heading downstairs.

As he did so, the harsh shriek of a drill disturbed him. He shook his head, trying to banish memories of the dentist and hoping the din wouldn't rouse Amy. Whoever was responsible, they were nearby; the racket grew louder as he reached the ground floor.

Rather than his laptop calling him, it was the cellar with its constant temperature and scientific equipment that attracted him today. With professional clinical trials underway, Erik rarely used the lab, but he occasionally dabbled. He wanted to try a new method of extracting the active ingredient from darria, and had brought some fresh leaves back from the allotment. Eager to begin, he opened the cellar door. To his surprise, it was unlocked, and electric light was already blazing at the foot of the stairs. What was going on? "Hello?" he called.

There was no reply. Erik descended the laminated steps, noting a fine powdery dust underfoot and a musty odour that overwhelmed the usual chip shop smell. The drill's whine increased in volume. Marty must have decided to carry out building work, yet another plan he'd failed to share. This was outrageous. The lab was supposed to be a sterile environment. Erik, typically even-tempered, was incandescent with rage. His anger totally overcame the nagging fear of a conversation with Marty about Kat's still.

At the foot of the stairs, Erik stared in horror at the sight before him. Kat's glass pipes and tanks were covered with the same red dust, as was Erik's lab equipment. A solitary workman in green overalls was standing by an industrial drill. The huge machine, about a metre in length, was mounted on metal plates which clanked and quivered as it bored a hole in the wall furthest from the stairs.

"Stop," Erik shouted, to no avail. The driller evidently couldn't hear him. Stepping forward, Erik shook the man's shoulders.

The operative flicked a switch, causing his machine to groan to a halt. He turned around. Although he wore a dust-mask and safety visor, Erik recognised him.

"Geoff?"

He didn't have a chance to say more. The alleged IT consultant rushed forward, fists at the ready, delivering a powerful blow to Erik's jaw. Caught off balance, Erik fell. Agony filled his head, and it occurred to him, in that split-second, that his crown had connected with the metal leg of his workbench. Mist filled his eyes, and he knew no more.

Erik awoke sprawled on the floor. He was almost grateful for the searing pain extending from ear to ear. After all, it proved he wasn't dead. Something was dreadfully amiss, though. His scalp felt wet and he could smell blood. His vision was blurred. He couldn't move.

Above him, Geoff's green-clad legs loomed, fuzzy and out of focus. "Jonno, I've never killed a man before," Geoff was saying.

There was no one else in the room. Erik realised Geoff was speaking on his phone. Time must have elapsed since he fell; how much, it was impossible to know.

"If I have to." Geoff sounded panicked. "You've got to help me get rid of it." He finished the conversation with a curt, "All right. Bye."

Fear almost blotted out the torment within Erik's skull. He was about to die, murdered like his parents. When had he last told Amy he loved her? Why had he never let Kat know he'd been besotted with his little sister from the minute she was born? It was too late. He'd no longer be there for them. The cancer research would stop. Without Erik's insistence on expensive clinical trials, Marty would make big money from teabags.

Fearing he was paralysed, Erik tried to shift into a standing position. It took an enormous effort, especially as he was trying to make no sound. He failed miserably, but only, he realised, because his hands and feet were bound. His relief was short-lived, as the movement attracted Geoff's attention once again.

"You're causing me all kinds of aggro," the older man grumbled. "Why did you have to pop up where you're not wanted?"

"Sorry," Erik said. Geoff had given him far more problems, but there was no point starting an argument. His single chance of staying alive was to get Geoff on his side.

"It's bad enough that I've had to fork out for a desk to get my hands on the keys," Geoff said. "I was told this place was derelict."

"It used to be," Erik said, remembering the days when he was the sole occupant of the building, paying a minimal rent to mind it while Marty sought planning permission for conversion. His speech was slurred, as if voiced by a phantom drifting into a nightmare. Perhaps this really was a dream. He hoped so. Belatedly, he recalled Geoff's words to Jonno, whoever that was. "You don't have to kill me," he mumbled. "I won't tell."

"Dead men tell no tales," Geoff said. He sighed. "I don't want to murder nobody. That's a whole new ballgame. You'd better hope my haul's a good one, and I can hop it over to Spain with the main man. Otherwise…" He drew a finger, or conceivably two, across his throat.

"What are you trying to do?" Erik asked.

"There's a tunnel under here," Geoff said. "and I can access the goldsmiths around the corner through it."

Erik's head whirled. He could sense Geoff was uncomfortable with the idea of killing him. There had to be a way of showing Geoff he was more valuable alive than dead. "I know more about those tunnels than anyone," he began.

Less than two years before, Erik had supervised Marty's refurbishment works. "There are communications tunnels below the entire Jewellery Quarter," Erik continued. "Access is prohibited to the public." His head throbbing, he could barely string both sentences together.

"Yes, I know that," Geoff snapped.

"Wait," Erik said. "That's not all. Yes, there was a shaft leading down to the tunnels. The door was where you're drilling." He was alert enough to grasp that someone had given Geoff that information. Who? A builder, an architect, or another villain? It didn't matter. "The shaft has been blocked. A load of concrete was poured into it." It had been a condition of the planning consent. Slurry was laboriously mixed in small quantities in the cobbled yard outside; it had taken days. Drilling through it would require even longer.

"Bad luck for me and worse luck for you, then," Geoff said.

Frantically, Erik racked his brains. "There's a jeweller's behind us," he offered. "Start drilling that way." He flapped a hand feebly, pointing to the wall on the left of the stairs.

"How do I know you're not leading me up the garden path?" Geoff demanded.

"I want to live," Erik replied. He fell silent, exhausted. It was true that the property backed onto an active workshop; what metals were used there, and whether Geoff would find anything valuable, he couldn't say.

Geoff hefted the drill into its new position, cursing. Erik, floating in and out of consciousness, wondered how long it would take his assailant to break through the wall. He coughed, choking on brick dust as the drill began to grind once more.

Chapter 15.   JERRY

On their return from Bruges the day before, Jerry and Scott had parked the white Transit in Jerry's lock-up. They hadn't bothered emptying the van, except for the crate of strong lager they split between them. The result was a Saturday morning hangover for Jerry, requiring plenty of coffee and cigarettes to restore his usual sunny nature. Once he felt human again, he, Scott and their cargo of booze headed for the Stow. It was just after eleven.

Dave, the first pub's landlord, had told his regulars they were on the way. The bootleggers did a roaring trade, paying Dave a hundred pounds from their takings. With a third of their stock gone, they set off for the next destination.

Scott didn't seem convinced they'd receive Bobby's promised warm welcome. "Look at the carpark," he grumbled, as Jerry turned the van into it. "Just a few old bangers, innit. That Volvo estate is so elderly, you wouldn't even nick it."

"Can I have a hubcap for my Volvo? Yep, that's a fair swap," Jerry mocked. "No worries, mate – whatever's left, we can sell in Ilford." It was his standard contingency plan, putting out the word to his network of friends and family, and sometimes a few of their fellow West Ham supporters. They achieved higher prices that way, but selling in small quantities took longer and was more of a gamble. You had to be careful who you approached. The Arsenal fans living next door were right out; one dissatisfied customer, and the Old Bill were on to you.

Leaving Scott to open the back of the van, Jerry entered the pub through its heavy swing door.

Bobby, tall and swarthy, was polishing glasses behind the bar. "We open for lunch in five minutes," he said, before recognising Jerry. "Oh, it's you. I'll let my mates know you're here."

"Where are they?" Jerry asked.

"Over there." Bobby gestured to a table in the farthest corner of the building. Around it were seated half a dozen or so men. Mostly young, they bore a certain physical resemblance to him; they could conceivably be his brothers or cousins.

The group's table was empty of drinks. Jerry felt predatory stares upon him. As he turned back to Bobby, the landlord's hand shook, dropping a glass. It smashed into several jagged pieces.

An alarming image of vampires floated into Jerry's mind. "We'll come back later when you've got a few more customers," he said.

"It won't be necessary," Bobby said. "They'll take whatever you've got."

Jerry nodded non-committally, returning to the car park. He found Scott rearranging their stock. There were a couple of boxes of spirits on the tarmac, while crates of pricier lagers had been left just within the Transit; the cheap stuff was behind it.

"I don't like this set-up," Jerry said, still uneasy. "Let's get out of here."

Before Scott could say a word, he pub door swung open, and several of Bobby's friends raced out at once. "Blimey, they're keen," Scott observed.

"Look again," Jerry shouted, slamming the Transit's rear doors shut.

"What are you doing?" Scott asked. Realisation dawned on his face. "They've got baseball bats," he said.

The pair were of one mind. Jerry sprinted to the driver's seat, employing the van's central locking as soon as Scott was sitting beside him. "Go, go, go," he shouted, starting the engine and putting the van in reverse.

"You're going to run over the Bacardi," Scott complained.

"Do you reckon we're taking it with us?" Jerry said. In his wing mirrors, he noticed two of their attackers diving to either side as the van lurched backwards. His satisfaction was short-lived. The men righted themselves, and with their fellows, began battering the van's windows.

"Drive forwards," Scott screamed, as the passenger window shattered, showering him with shards of glass.

"Not yet," Jerry replied. Adrenaline coursed through him. He'd teach the gang a lesson. They might think their bats gave them the upper hand, but he controlled the biggest weapon of all. He applied his foot to the accelerator, nearly sending the vehicle into one of the bangers parked behind it.

The robbers were in front of them now, about to target the windscreen with their clubs.

"They couldn't resist," Jerry murmured. "I knew it." Its engine roaring, the Transit sped forward. With a thud, two of the young men toppled under the van, their friends scattering to one side. "Got them," Jerry said, a smirk on his face. "That'll show those vampires."

"Vampires?" Scott looked at him enquiringly as the van raced into the road and away at speed.

Jerry shrugged. "The bloodsuckers come from Transylvania, don't they? That's in Romania, where Bobby's from, and the rest of them too, I bet."

"I told you we couldn't rely on Jon Halloran," Scott whined. "He needs to sort them out."

"Too true," Jerry said. "He can get the van repaired as well. New window, new panels, new tyres. There'll be blood on these."

"New plates," Scott chipped in. "You'll want to send off the old log book to the DVLA; say you've sold it to Mr Michael Mouse."

"Right," Jerry agreed. "Fancy a drink back at mine? Grab a Duvel or two out of the back?" He needed it. The ambush had unnerved him more than he cared to admit. If Jon couldn't keep the foreign gangs off their backs, what was the point of working for him?

Chapter 16.   ERIK

"Erik!" He heard Amy calling his name in the distance. Too late, Erik remembered their plans for a weekend away.

Geoff ceased his labours for a moment.

"Down here, love, if you know what's good for you," the robber growled.

"But I don't understand," Amy was saying.

"Shut up," Geoff barked, adding, "I should have locked that door."

There was the sound of a scuffle, and a scream abruptly cut short.

Erik's heart missed a beat. He wriggled his hands and feet, trying to shift and see what was happening, fearing the worst and hoping only that she'd survived.

"Don't make a sound," Geoff said, "or I'll have to kill you."

"What have you done to Erik?" she asked, the words emerging in a hoarse whisper.

"That's better, love," Geoff said. "Now I'll just tie you up, and you can sit over there, nice and quiet."

"What about Erik?" she repeated. "There's blood all over him." She sounded hysterical. "He needs a doctor. Please…"

"Later," Geoff said, his tone sharp.

Erik could see her now, or at any rate, a hazy blue outline of the jeans and jumper she'd set aside for the day when she'd been packing. That had been a last-minute job, accomplished swiftly with cocktail-fuelled certainty. Their pleasant evening in the pub seemed like months ago.

Geoff's phone resounded with a Sex Pistols riff. "Hello? Hit a snag," he said, anxiety apparent in his voice. "It's like Clapham Junction down here. Speak to you later." Then, returning to the task at hand, he said, "No more arguing, you silly tart."

Erik heard a stifled "ouch" and an intake of breath as Geoff secured a rope around Amy's wrists and ankles. Finally, she was left in a seated position, propped against Erik's workbench.

Geoff switched on the drill. As its screeching intensified, Erik realised Geoff was effectively deaf. The crook wouldn't hear anything he and Amy said to each other. Of course, the clatter of the machine was such that they might not either. "Amy?" he yelled.

"Erik," she hollered back, following it with a huge sob. "I thought you were out cold, maybe even dead."

89

It was possible they'd both perish if they couldn't escape from the cellar. He didn't want to alarm her by giving voice to his suspicions. "Are you okay?" he ventured.

She was still weeping. "No," she bellowed, panic audible as she added, "But what about you?"

"I'm fine," he lied, a spark of hope flickering in his addled, aching brain. "Amy – has he left his phone on that bench?"

He heard a series of thuds. "I can't get upright to see," she said, her words emerging between sobs, "but I'll shake the table, because if the phone is there, it may fall off."

Geoff continued to drill, unheeding as further thumps, bumps and crashes followed. A number of small objects flew off the bench. Most, if not all, would be Erik's lab equipment. Verging on delirium, he found he didn't care what happened to it any more.

The ear-splitting cacophony of the drill seemed to recede. At the same time, Erik began to shiver. He felt his head might burst. As if from afar, he heard Amy's voice. What was she saying? She had something. Now she wanted police and ambulance. That was a good idea, he thought, as he slipped into oblivion.

Chapter 17.   SHAUN

As a free man, Shaun would never have chosen to use a mobile phone routinely stored in a junkie's bottom. However, different rules applied in Belmarsh. When he shook Adam Bartlett's hand in the exercise yard, he knew exactly what he was about to receive.

Young Bartlett was a key man in Shaun's network, a prisoner prepared to keep drugs and phones safe in return for the means to feed his habit. The small mobile he palmed to Shaun was protected by a plastic ziplock bag. Shaun was under no illusions about its usual hiding place.

His anticipation was high, albeit not enough to merit taking risks. He waited until, armed with his cleaning kit, he could visit the shower block. There, he was safe from CCTV and the sound of running water would mask his conversation from passing screws. He still needed to keep a watchful eye for them, of course.

He jabbed at the phone's tiny, plasticky keys, waiting for Jon to answer before speaking.

"Hello." Jon's voice sounded nervous.

"It's Dad. How much did he lift?"

"Nothing, Dad. The filth nicked him. That's the end of his parole, isn't it? He'll be back to Belmarsh again."

"No way." Nausea gripped Shaun, his dreams of a life-changing heist coming to an abrupt end. He'd needed the cash to make a new start as soon as he could escape. It was bad news for Jonesy as well; the jewel thief would be back inside for years. "What happened?"

"I don't know. Jonesy's brief called me, but he wouldn't tell me everything," Jon said. "There was some girl."

Shaun pursed his lips. There had been a girl, too, when he'd been caught in those tunnels: Kat. Was it too much of a coincidence to believe she would thwart his plans again?

"If you ask me," Jon said, "Jonesy was grassed up to the Old Bill by his mates inside. The brief said as much."

"Who?" Shaun asked.

"You tell me," Jon said. "Who knew we were planning it?"

Shaun recalled the silent gambler, Kemble. Apparently absorbed in mathematical puzzles, he'd heard enough to be aware a theft was in prospect. Although the fine detail had been communicated by Jon to Geoff Jones later, it wouldn't take a genius to join the dots. Then there was the Welshman, Tyler Williams, listening outside the cell. "Leave that one with me," he said. "Anything else I should know?"

"Only Anton," Jon said. "He's refusing point blank to supply any more."

"Take care of the old hippy like we agreed," Shaun said. "Problems on the outside are your job. I'll deal with the cons inside."

He didn't know which of the two inmates had grassed, or if indeed either of them had done so. Perhaps Kat was responsible for the fiasco after all. He couldn't afford to take a chance, though. Both Williams and Kemble needed to be reminded that informing wouldn't be tolerated.

Williams was the easier target. It was twenty four hours until payday, so the Welshman would be short of tobacco. Jenner was bound to be his first port of call.

"Jens," Shaun asked, as they sat in their cell with the evening meal, a lurid yellow soup masquerading as chicken curry, "Do you have an assignation with Tyler Williams tonight?"

Jenner winced. "Not an assignation, as such," he said. "I'm expecting him to visit for a chat later."

"I'll stick around for him," Shaun said. He'd usually spend the evening association period outside the cell, seeing to business, but there was time enough for that afterwards.

Jenner looked uncomfortable. "I rather hoped he and I could speak in private."

"Do whatever you like," Shaun said. "I want words with him first."

Jenner shrugged. He evidently knew better than to refuse. "Cup of tea?" he asked.

Shaun assented, watching as Jenner busied himself with their little kettle. "I'll refill that," he said, once the brew was made.

"I was saving the milk for later," Jenner protested. Neither of them had any time for the creamer that was supplied in the tea pack; they retained a carefully measured amount of breakfast milk to use throughout the day.

"I'm not making another," Shaun said, holding the kettle under the tap. He set it to one side without switching it on. Jens seemed puzzled. He'd learn.

It wasn't long before Tyler Williams arrived, standing hesitantly on the threshold of the cell.

"Come in," Shaun invited him.

Williams grimaced. "I thought we'd be alone," he said to Jenner.

"Soon, my boy," Jenner said, ushering him into the room. "My friend just wanted a word first."

Shaun picked up the kettle, immediately clocking the fear in Williams' eyes. He poured the ice-cold contents over the Welshman.

Jenner's jaw fell. "What did you do that for?" he gasped.

Shaun ignored him. "That was a warning," he said to Williams. "Don't ever grass me up. The next time, it'll be a proper jugging." The kettle would be boiling, with sugar in it so the hot liquid stuck to the skin. Apart from naïve newcomers like Jenner, all prisoners knew this. Tyler Williams, by his reaction, was no exception.

"I've never..." Williams began.

"Shut it," Shaun said. "I don't know you. None of us do. You were shipped in from Cardiff all of a sudden. You could be a nonce for all I know. Your paperwork says you're a blagger, but it could have been faked. Count yourself lucky. I'm giving you a second chance." It wasn't unknown for the authorities to provide sex offenders with false documents. No right-thinking criminal would tolerate their presence on the wing if they knew the truth. That was how such prisoners were blackmailed into becoming informants.

Shaun supposed he could have asked Ed Rothery if this was the case, but Rothery wouldn't necessarily know, or be truthful.

Jenner was apoplectic. "This is extreme," he protested. "My young friend simply wishes to be allowed to smoke, which is his basic human right."

"I've told it like it is," Shaun said. "All he has to do is behave himself. Anyway," he was a lot calmer now, "I'll leave you two to 'chat'. Or whatever."

He left to mete out the same treatment to Kemble, having first issued a judicious threat to the gambler's new cellmate to make himself scarce until bang-up.

Kemble took the dunking, administered using his own kettle, with dead eyes. "I won't let you down," he said to Shaun. "I need my skag, don't I?"

That made sense, and Shaun almost regretted his haste. Still, a chill ran down his spine when he pondered on Kemble's distant eyes. His unease vanished on returning to his cell. Jenner was in a foul mood, and not shy to share the reason.

"Williams is invoking Rule 45," Jenner said gloomily, "whatever that is, but it means he's going to be segregated. I've just helped him with his application."

"Oh dear, Jens, are you going to miss your toy boy?" Shaun said. He regarded Williams' action as vindicating his threat, and therefore had no sympathy for the MP.

Jenner gave him a filthy look, switching on the television and pointedly making a single cup of tea.

Chapter 18.   MARTY

Marty faced a dilemma. A hospital visit was neither the time nor place to shout at Erik about the illegal still in Leopold Passage. Anyway, although he was seething at the discovery, he was nevertheless worried about Erik's welfare. As ever, he tried to defuse the tension with a joke. "This is all about avoiding your in-laws, isn't it?" he said to Erik.

Erik didn't reply. He was paler than ever. A row of stitches ran across his forehead and into the hairline, part of which had been shaved. Below it, his green eyes were glazed, staring out of the window. His hospital cubicle had a view over treetops and roofs to hills in the distance. A jug of water and a glass rested on the table next to him, together with a lunchtime sandwich, untouched. There was also a paperback, its title emblazoned in bold Cyrillic letters. Marty recognised it a dystopian novel by Erik's favourite Russian writer, Vladimir Sorokin. It looked shiny, unopened, unread.

Marty abandoned attempts at conversation. "I've been down to the cellar," he said. "It really is a mess. Lumps of brick and dust all over the place. And a load of pipes and vessels." Despite the fine red powder covering them, it was obvious what they were. "Oh yes," Marty continued. "They look just like the contraptions I've seen at the Snow Mountain factory. There's an overpowering smell of booze, too. Rough, undrinkable slops, in my opinion." Despite his good intentions, fury smouldered. He glared at Erik. "The kit isn't yours, is it? It belongs to your sister, I bet. Am I right?"

Mutely, Erik nodded.

Marty's lip curled. "What were you thinking of?" he said, anger adding menace to his voice even though he didn't raise it. "She's making poteen, moonshine; call it what you will. It's dangerous. The stuff's flammable. You, of all people, should know that." He was aware of blood rushing to his head. No doubt his face was scarlet. "You put my property at risk, Erik. I deserved better from you."

"Sorry," Erik whispered.

"I was nearly on the wrong end of a police investigation," Marty raged. "Keeping an unlicensed still is a serious matter."

"She's applied for a licence," Erik said.

"Even so, I want her out of there right away," Marty commanded, "and that heap of junk with her. Do you understand?"

"Yes," Erik said, his voice so subdued it could scarcely be heard.

"See to it," Marty said. The fire was beginning to leave him. "I need you back soon," he added, uneasily aware of his dependence on his business partner and starting to regret ranting so much. "When will you be out?"

"I don't know," Erik said, his words devoid of inflection.

"Your nurses seem to think you'll be home in a couple of days," Marty said. He'd given them a box of Quality Street on his arrival in the ward; they'd repaid him with a chat about Erik's prognosis.

"Maybe," Erik replied, unenthusiastically.

"Erik, can I help?" Marty asked, increasingly concerned.

"It's nothing to do with you. You can't do anything." At last, Erik spoke with passion. "I couldn't save her." His voice sounded thick, almost drunk.

"Who do you mean?" Marty asked. "Kat?" It was his best guess, especially now he'd seen the still. Kat and trouble always seemed to find each other, and like everyone else, her older brother was left to pick up the pieces.

"Amy," Erik replied. "I couldn't protect her in the cellar. She was only there because of me. Her life was in danger, but I was helpless."

Marty shook his head. "Why worry?" he said. "Amy's okay. She was able to get to a phone and call the police."

"No thanks to me," Erik said. "I wasn't there for her."

"Snap out of it," Marty said. "She's fine. Trust me. She's even said she'll clean up your lab equipment." Amy wasn't the whiny millennial he'd imagined when they first met, and he was glad now that he'd offered her a job. Maybe he should give her time off work to see Erik. He should persuade Angela to visit, too. She was better at dispensing tea and sympathy than her husband.

Rising from his visitor's chair, Marty clapped a hand on Erik's shoulder. "You'll soon be right as rain. I've arranged a meeting with a cannabis farmer next week, and I'd like you to be there."

"What?" Shock was written on Erik's face.

"Yes, that feature in the HuffPost really made waves," Marty said. "I've been approached by three national newspapers, so darria tea is going to get a mountain of free publicity. And a cannabis farmer phoned me this morning. He's about an hour's drive away, with a large plot which he can grub up for darria cultivation. You know, maybe I'll buy the land." He'd make sure it was cleared, and zoned for agricultural use, of course.

"No way," Erik said. "I left a message for you. We shouldn't get involved with people like that. I thought you were keen to stay on the right side of the law."

"Whatever the guy's done in the past, cultivating darria is legal," Marty said. "Unlike operating a still without a licence. Anyway, what else can I do? There's so much interest in darria tea now, we have to grow more of it, and fast. Unfortunately, every time I've put in an offer on a farm, I've been outbid."

"You could try paying more," Erik said.

"I never overpay," Marty pointed out.

"Don't I know it?" Erik said. "Shouldn't I have a say? It's my business too."

Marty's anger simmered once more. He'd expected some debate, but not a total lack of compromise. Erik shouldn't be telling him what to do. Who was paying for Darria Enterprises? Confronted by his business partner's obstinacy, Marty would have to meet the prospective darria farmer alone. "I've got to go now," he told Erik coldly.

As he returned to the Jag, Marty brooded on Erik's reaction. The young man had been unusually argumentative. Perhaps the blow to his head had left more than physical scars.

Chapter 19.   SHAUN

Baptised a Roman Catholic, Shaun had spent most of his life avoiding church services unless his presence was required for a wedding or funeral. On admission to Belmarsh, however, he'd given his faith as Church of England. Every Sunday, he attended Anglican mass in the prison chapel, a rare chance to mix with cons from other wings of the prison.

The chapel was a circular hall with exposed brown brick walls, which to Shaun's mind gave it an unfinished look. It boasted little in the way of decoration: an ecumenical space, it was designed to allow different religious banners to be unfurled as men of various faiths filed in and out. The prisoners were assembled on rows of cheap meeting-room chairs. Shaun, strategically seated in the middle, watched Marshall Jenner at the front nodding in agreement at the priest's sermon.

The congregation stood to say the creed. "We believe in one God," Shaun began. "What happened, Jonesy?" His voice was soft; swamped by the prayers of the faithful, it was inaudible except to those nearby.

Geoff Jones, standing to the left of Shaun, squirmed. "It wasn't derelict," he mumbled. "In fact, there were people in and out of the place like Clapham Junction. I've told your boy all that."

There was a tap on Shaun's shoulder. "All right," he said, putting out a hand behind him. Someone handed him a scrap of paper. He read the message on it, a scrawled list of suggested prices for heroin, ecstasy and mamba. "That's fine," he said, giving a thumbs up. "I'll pass it on." He nudged the man on his right.

A screw was glancing in his direction. "For our sake, he was crucified," Shaun intoned. His business was mostly done. He waited for the prison officer to look away, then turned to Jonesy again. "I handed that job to you on a plate," he said, injecting a note of pure ice into his words. "You should have planned it better. I'd watch your step if I were you." When revenge was delivered, he wanted Jonesy to know why.

"Wait," Geoff Jones said. "That blonde girl was there. Kat. Don't you want to know more?"

Was the Pope Catholic? "Yes," Shaun said, careful not to appear too eager. Animosity forgotten, he said, "Tell me everything, Jonesy."

Chapter 20.   **KAT**

The buzzer sounded, jolting Kat out of a deep sleep. It felt stupidly early, although she'd returned home straight after her shift yesterday. Tim was in London, visiting Mayfair clubs and five star hotels. Ruefully, he'd told her that he'd be staying in a Travelodge on the North Circular for a week. It was a far cry from the swanky hotels and business class flights his father enjoyed.

Already, Kat longed for Tim's return, even though he'd promised to see potential investors while in London. The destruction of the still needn't hold them back, he'd said; as soon as they'd raised enough cash, Kat could build a new one just as they'd planned. It was refreshing to meet a member of the Bridges family who really believed in her, and was so cute too. Tim was almost too good to be true.

Daylight was creeping around the curtains and her phone revealed it was after nine. Pressing the button to speak, she asked who it was.

"Post for you."

Kat dragged a filmy negligée of the palest green around her shoulders, tying it hastily as she dashed barefoot down two flights of stairs to the ground floor.

"Sign here, Miss."

"That's not for me."

The young postman persuaded her to sign anyway. Most of the items were for Erik and the freelance workers who rented desks on the ground floor. Usually, her brother would be up and about, but he'd been in hospital for more than a week now. She decided to take his post there later, leaving the rest on a shelf in the lobby.

There was just one letter for her, with a London postmark, the address written in a semi-legible scrawl and using the minimum words necessary to have it delivered: Kat, 3 Leopold Passage, Birmingham.

Back in the flat, she opened it. The contents sent a chill down her spine.

Who could have sent such a letter? Only Erik, Amy and Tim knew where she lived. Marty might suspect, of course, but he didn't know for sure. Erik had owned up to the distilling equipment, but not to giving his sister lodgings. Anyway, why would Marty call her a slut and threaten to kill her? If he really hated her so much, he'd had plenty of opportunity to do something about it in the past. Whatever their differences, he'd never been anything other than courteous towards her.

Erik, ten years older, had been a rock to her all her life, his support constant and unfailing. His head injury hadn't changed his kindness and devotion to her; he was still risking Marty's wrath by offering her a home. He couldn't have been anywhere near London to post a letter, either. Despite Amy's recent frostiness, she, too, had been a loyal friend for years and was beyond suspicion.

That left Tim, Kat's perfect lover. The notion seemed fantastical. Nervously, Kat chewed her lip until she tasted the sharp tang of blood.

Chapter 21.   MARTY

As a teenager, Marty had lovingly restored a decrepit BSA Bantam motorbike and taken it to the Glastonbury music festival. That was the last time he'd encountered someone like Anton Dimmock.

They'd made an appointment to meet at 10am at Marty's warehouse, not far from the centre of Birmingham. Marty would have been the first to admit that the premises were functional rather than smart, but at least they could have a discussion in private.

Absorbed in paperwork that morning, Marty didn't look at the clock until ten fifteen. He phoned his secretary. "Any sign of Anton, Tanya?"

"Nothing," she reported. "Do you think he's lost?" They were barely half a mile from New Street station, but Anton was driving. It wasn't unknown for visitors to become disorientated in the city's busy highways.

"He'll have a satnav," Marty said. "It must be the traffic."

By eleven, he'd begun to wonder if he'd been mistaken about the date. He tried phoning Anton's mobile, the sole means of communication with the farmer, but couldn't reach him. Finally, at twenty past eleven, Tanya phoned to say she had ZZ Top waiting in the reception lobby.

Marty felt this was harsh, as Tanya herself favoured interesting hairstyles in improbable colours. Today, she'd shaped her locks into a sea-green bob. He knew exactly what she meant, however, as soon as he clapped eyes on Anton. The farmer's hair and beard, a mousy shade streaked with grey, reached down to his chest. He was wearing a tatty grey parka, faded blue jeans and jumper, and brown Dr Martens boots. A smell of sandalwood and tobacco clung to him, alongside another aroma with which Marty had recently reacquainted himself.

"Anton. Good to see you." Marty held out his hand. After a moment's hesitation, his visitor took it, displaying a firm grip.

"So this is what big business looks like." Anton cast mild blue eyes around the square, white-painted lobby, resting on the prominent No Smoking sign. "Mind if I light up?"

"I do, actually," Marty said. "That notice is there for a reason. It's illegal to smoke in here. You're welcome to go outside." He didn't claim to be a fan of health and safety legislation, but he wasn't keen on nicotine either.

Given his profession, Anton undoubtedly had a more relaxed attitude to rules. However, he obediently said he would wait outside for five minutes. Marty watched him roll a cigarette, standing next to a Land Rover as scruffy as its owner, and probably of a similar vintage. Perhaps Anton didn't possess a satnav after all.

Tanya brought a tray of hot drinks and shortbread before fetching Anton.

"Sit down," Marty said. "I expect you'd like coffee? How do you take it? Help yourself to biscuits."

"I'll have it black, please," Anton said.

"I'm afraid the delay means we can only spare you an hour. I have a lunch appointment," Marty said. It was a convenient lie, intended to keep his visitor focused during their meeting. "I suggest I describe what Darria Enterprises wants to achieve, then you'll have a chance to explain what you can do for us."

Already munching on a shortbread finger, Anton nodded.

"I'm in partnership with a scientist from Bazakistan. He's spent half his life researching darria, a shrub that grows there."

"It's not all that grows in Bazakistan, is it?" Anton said. "That's where dope comes from."

"Yes, the growing conditions are similar," Marty said. "Naturally, the properties of the plants are different. You may not have heard much about darria, but it has a lot of potential."

"Teabags for rich old ladies," Anton interjected.

"I'll tell my wife you said that," Marty replied. "She was so excited to see her picture in the HuffPost. Less impressed that her age was published."

"She's aged better than you," Anton said.

"Exactly," Marty said, refusing to take offence. "Darria has caused a stir among my wife's friends. In fact, it was one of her ladies who lunch that wrote the Huffington Post feature. We think we can make money from darria teabags as a dietary supplement for ladies who'd like to preserve their looks." He grinned. "My wife is quite the poster girl. But anyway, we're using that money to develop a new cancer drug from darria."

It was hard to detect Anton's stance behind his beard, but his tone was sceptical. "Here, in Birmingham – in this shed?"

Marty frowned. "I think my warehouse is a bit better than a shed, actually. But yes, it's just Erik and me, although we're paying another

102

company a fortune to run clinical trials. That's the closest we'll get to Big Pharma. Selling out to them isn't part of the plan."

"Cool," Anton gasped. "Stick it to the Man." He leaned forward, smiling and clearly excited. "I can grow the stuff for you, no problem."

"You grow cannabis, right?" Marty asked.

"I certainly do," Anton said. "Good quality, two crops a year. Never had any complaints." He beamed. "You say darria thrives in similar conditions, so I'm definitely your man. It's a less risky crop, know what I mean?"

"Indeed," Marty said. "It's entirely legal. As long as the land is zoned for agricultural use. I take it yours is?"

"It must be. I haven't heard otherwise," Anton said.

"Okay, I'll come along and see it," Marty said. "You said you'd be open to offers for the land."

"I could be, but don't you want me to grow darria for you?" Anton asked. "How much do you put in a tea bag – three grammes? They're a pound each, so that's ten pounds for an ounce of dried leaves. I could sell them to you for half that, and you'd make a tidy profit."

Anton's arithmetic was faultless, but his calculations hopelessly optimistic. "I'd make a loss," Marty stated. "There are processing costs, retail and wholesale margins, and tax to pay. I'd rather buy the land and grow darria myself."

"You need someone like me to do it," Anton protested.

The more Marty listened, the less inclined he was to do business with the hippy. "I'll tell it to you straight," he said. "I know there's no special skill involved in growing cannabis."

Anton bristled.

"Let me finish," Marty said. "Back in the day, my friends had a few plants, for personal use. If they could grow it, anyone can. Darria's the same." Erik might disagree, he knew. "When I told the HuffPost I'd like to meet a marijuana farmer, it was a soundbite, that's all. It got me publicity, which was what I wanted. I don't need you. If you're not really interested in selling up, I don't know why you came here."

"I want to get away from cannabis," Anton said, his voice subdued. "Well, except for personal use." He stared into space for what seemed like a day, although it was no more than five minutes. "I suppose you could take a look," he conceded.

"What's your price?" Marty asked. Experience had taught him never to table the first amount in a negotiation.

"Twenty thousand pounds," Anton said airily.

It sounded suspiciously cheap, unless the hippy's fields were the size of a postage stamp.

"Come around any time," Anton said. "This afternoon, if you like. It's not signposted – I mean, in my line of work, it wouldn't be – but I've brought a map." He pulled a piece of folded paper from the pocket of his parka. It was a torn-off extract from an Ordnance Survey map. "Look, X marks the spot."

It was in the middle of a wood, at the end of what appeared to be a path leading from a minor road. Marty traced a finger over it. "How will I get there by car?" he asked.

"My Land Rover eats that track," Anton replied. "If all you've got is a Jag, you'll need to walk from the lane. Bring wellies."

"It's in the middle of nowhere," Marty said.

"Not at all," Anton told him, pointing to a smudge right on the map's ragged edge. "That's Dunstable, that is."

Marty had a vague idea that Dunstable was a market town on the old coaching route to London. He didn't revise his opinion. "I can't fit it in today, but I'll see you tomorrow afternoon," he said. "Two o'clock."

"Cool," Anton agreed. His enthusiasm seemed to have returned. He handed the map to Marty before stuffing three shortbread fingers into his pocket.

"I'll get my lawyer to draw up a contract," Marty said.

Anton blanched. "We don't need paperwork, do we?"

"I'm afraid we do," Marty told him. "I'm not spending money until I can be sure what I'm getting for it." He rose to his feet. "Sorry, it's nearly twelve thirty. I'll see you tomorrow."

As Tanya showed the hippy out, Marty almost picked up the phone to Erik. The conversation with Anton had rung a peal of alarm bells. It was the thought of admitting he'd been wrong that stayed Marty's hand. Curiosity was nagging him too. Despite his qualms, he knew that he would, after all, drive to the Bedfordshire countryside the next day.

Chapter 22.   **JERRY**

They met Jon at a pub in Finsbury Park. None of them had visited it before, and they didn't intend to do so again. They travelled on unregistered Oyster cards. Jerry's van was being quietly repaired by one of Jon's cousins, a qualified mechanic.

Jerry and Scott were on the Duvel, for which they'd acquired a taste after four years of bootlegging. Jon was drinking Guinness. Beneath his trim beard, young Jon looked just like his father had, back in the days when they'd go for a drink after a match at the Boleyn ground: his face thin, pale and sharp, his eyes a startling light blue within a fringe of black lashes.

Shaun's eyes had always been hard, a warning to stay on the right side of him. He'd been prepared to fight anyone, using his fists and worse on visiting fans, villains who strayed out of line, and others who simply argued too much. Now, Jerry wondered if his son would show the same mettle.

Scott was the first to ask. "What are you going to do about those Romanians?" he demanded in a truculent tone.

Jon raised his eyebrows. "I've taken care of Bobby," he said. "Don't you watch the news?"

"Must have missed it," Scott muttered. "Do tell."

"He's in intensive care," Jon said. "Knife in the back. Good enough?"

Jerry tried not to gawp. He thought Scott was going to argue, and nudged the smaller man in warning. Jon's eyes followed the movement.

Scott simply said, "It's a start."

"I'm doing a lot for you," Jon said coldly. "I need you to do something for me. You know Anton Dimmock?"

"Doesn't ring a bell," Jerry said, and Scott, too, looked blank.

"As I thought," Jon said. "He's an old hippy who lives out in the sticks. I want to talk to him, but he doesn't seem keen. You guys can bring him into London for me."

"You're having a laugh," Jerry objected. "I haven't got my wheels back. Any road, if he's avoiding you, he won't want to come with us, will he?"

"That's where you're wrong," Jon said. "I've got something for you that he'll find very, very persuasive. And it doesn't even involve violence."

Chapter 23.   MARTY

Dunstable turned out to be one of the depressing dormitory settlements that encircled London, its grubby brick edges blurring into the next town. It was a short, easy drive from the M1 motorway. Anton's farm was harder to find. Marty drove through the market town, heading up a steep hill on its outskirts before turning onto a potholed country lane. It gradually narrowed to the extent he prayed he wouldn't meet oncoming traffic. Tall trees either side were bursting with spring growth, their branches meeting at the top to form a claustrophobic green tunnel. Although no other cars or people were visible, he had an eerie sensation of being watched.

Eventually, he spotted a muddy track to his left, barred with a huge metal gate. Slowing down, Marty saw a wooden sign on which had been painted an Alsatian's head and the legend: "Dangerous Dogs – Keep Out." There was no indication this was a farm. Uncertain if it was Anton's property, Marty continued along the lane. His arrival at a crossroads with a public house in one quadrant told him he'd travelled too far. Turning back, he parked next to the gate, hoping his Jag wouldn't become stuck in the mire.

Marty changed into wellington boots to walk down the track. Unfortunately, the gate was locked, and he couldn't find gaps in the wire mesh fence on either side.

"Anton," he called. He continued to feel staring eyes upon him, but nobody, either human or canine, responded. Marty tried the hippy's mobile phone, again without a reply. Hoping he'd found the right place, he climbed over the gate, tramping along the trail towards the heart of the woods.

Despite the dense trees and murky light, the way ahead was clear enough: rutted and pitted with reassuring signs of the Land Rover's passage. Marty was still aware of being observed, the feeling intensifying as he marched further into the forest. An animal bounded across his path in a blurry flash. He had the sense of a giant rabbit or small kangaroo, both the stuff of nightmares rather than a mid-afternoon stroll in the English countryside.

His anxiety was lessened as he recalled that, back at his office, Tanya knew where he was going. He could defend himself in a fight, too. In his youth, Marty has been a capable amateur boxer. Like riding a bicycle or drinking strong ale, it was a skill that once mastered, was never lost.

He'd been walking for over ten minutes, past more placards urging him to stay away, when he spied Anton's Land Rover. Discoloured with rust, moss edging the windows, its presence in the forest seemed as natural as the trees around it. Hurrying towards it, Marty saw the vehicle was parked in front of a clearing little bigger than his garden in Wellington Road. It was surrounded by a brambly hedge and a rough fence around a metre high: three parallel strands of wire supported by timber posts. To one side, there was a substantial gate, fashioned from wood. Fantastical heads – bearded men, monsters with tusks, and unicorns – were carved into the gate and the top of each post.

Squinting through gaps in the hedge, Marty saw the cultivated area contained no trees. He recognised the cannabis bushes thriving within it, however. Anton hadn't lied about his prowess. He was, however, nowhere in sight. Marty checked his watch. It was five to two.

Just beyond the ornate gate was a ramshackle shed, a construction of wood and corrugated boards covered in moss. It reminded Marty of television documentaries about shanty towns. Might Anton be there? Marty jabbed at his phone again.

The blast of an old Nokia ringtone could be heard from within the Land Rover. The driver's door opened, and Anton emerged, staggering drowsily. "Sorry, man, I was snatching forty winks," he said.

"You wanted to show me the farm," Marty said. "I thought it would be bigger than this."

"It's a smallholding," Anton replied, without missing a beat. "Anyway," he gestured expansively, "I own twenty acres of woodlands. If we need more room for darria, I'll cut down a few more trees."

"Aren't they protected?" Marty asked, his misgivings increasing.

"Who's going to notice?" Anton said. "No-one has yet."

Three or four sandy-coloured animals, appearing as if from nowhere, hopped over to the farmer. Like the creature Marty had seen earlier, they resembled tall, stretched-out rabbits with long tails.

"Hello?" Marty said.

"Wallabies," Anton told him. He stroked one of the creatures. "My friends."

"Your pets?" Marty asked.

"No," Anton replied. "They're wild. A couple of marsupials escaped from Whipsnade Zoo fifty years ago, and now a huge pack roams the forest. Usually a wallaby wouldn't come near a human being – they're quite shy – but they make an exception for me. I give them the weeds when I've had a tidy-up."

"But if you're attracting them here, won't they eat your marijuana plants?" Marty said. "That fence doesn't look very solid."

"Oh, it does the job," Anton said. "There's ten thousand volts going through it. You didn't expect that, did you do? Nor do the wallabies."

"Too right I didn't expect it. There are no warning signs," Marty said. "No power lines either."

"I'm off-grid," Anton said smugly, "but I've rigged up wind and solar energy."

"Thanks for the tour," Marty said. He'd seen enough. It was time to make his excuses and leave.

Anton's smirk vanished, replaced by a panicked expression. "You tricked me," he accused.

"What?" Puzzled, Marty looked behind him, seeing two policemen walking down the path. Despite the gravity of the situation, he almost burst out laughing. One tall, the other short, they called to mind a comedy double act.

"It's a sting," Anton said, his eyes wild. "You've brought the filth."

"Nothing to do with me," Marty said grimly. "I'm as worried as you are." How was he going to explain his presence at a cannabis farm? His flash car wouldn't impress; on the contrary, it would provoke more interest.

Anton took no notice. He brought a key out of his pocket, unchaining the gate and pushing it wide open. "Here," he said to the wallabies, "Eat up."

Marty assumed it was a last-ditch attempt to destroy the evidence. The marsupials rose to the occasion, jumping into the field and grazing on the juicy young growth.

The police officers were upon them now. "I suppose you know why we're here, Mr Dimmock," the tall one said to Anton. "Our boss wants to see you for questioning."

Anton desperately extemporised. "I'm not Dimmock," he said, pointing to Marty. "He is."

Marty's jaw dropped. "I think I can prove I'm not, officer," he said, removing his driving licence from his wallet. "Let me assure you, I'm not involved in anything illegal. I'm here on business."

"I'm sure you are," the taller man said, sniggering.

"We were only supposed to bring in the old hippy, Jerry," the short policeman said. "What are we going to do with the other one?"

"I'll ask the, er, Chief Inspector," the man called Jerry replied. "Put the cuffs on them."

For an instant, Marty froze, overcome by panic. A year ago, he'd been kidnapped in Bazakistan, handcuffed and held for a week in a cramped cell. He sweated, his heart pounding, as the short man advanced on him. Instinct told him the strangers weren't policemen. Despite his terror, his voice was firm as he challenged the pair. "Where's your ID?" he asked. "You haven't read me my rights. I don't even know why you're arresting me."

"Drugs, innit," the small policeman said.

Marty took flight, sprinting towards the road in his ungainly wellingtons. No identification would be forthcoming, that much was clear. He didn't care who Jerry and his comrade were, or what their endgame might be. Evading capture was his only goal.

"Go after him, Scott," he heard Jerry say. "I'll deal with the hippy."

The road was perhaps half a mile distant along the rough track. Running as fast as the furrowed mud permitted, it seemed to take Marty a lifetime to return to the metal gate. He looked longingly at his Jaguar on the other side.

Behind him, Scott was a few yards away. There was no time to climb to freedom before the small man would be upon him. Marty turned and charged at his opponent, his right fist swinging upwards towards the man's nose.

There was a cracking sound as the blow connected. Scott yelped, clutching his face. Blood was streaming down his lips and chin, splashing onto his fake uniform.

Seizing his chance, Marty scrambled over the gate, jumping into the Jag. He engaged central locking and started the engine.

He saw the Transit double-parked alongside his car, and realised escape would be harder than he'd thought. There was but a narrow gap. As Marty assessed his chances of clearing it, Jerry dropped down from the gate and dashed into the white van.

Marty accelerated through the channel before Jerry could close it, missing the other vehicle by a whisker. He managed to start on his journey just as the Transit sprang into life. As he'd feared, the white van loomed in his rear-view mirror. Marty applied pedal to the metal, feeling the G-force as his three litre V6 engine rose to the challenge.

Another glance at the mirror told him the van was diminishing in size. He knew it would be. Nothing could match his coupé's superior acceleration and cornering ability. This, above all, was why he'd chosen such a handsome devil of a car. By the time he arrived in Dunstable, the Transit was nowhere in sight.

Chapter 24.   JERRY

"How come you lost him?" Scott grumbled. The words were nasal and indistinct. Scott's nose was red, puffy and ballooning in size. The metallic scent of fresh blood clung to him.

Jerry sighed. "This isn't a sportscar. Who cares, anyway? He's just some guy wanting a drugs deal. He won't be talking about us, and we won't be talking about him. Jon asked us to fetch the hippy, and that's what we're doing."

"You should have put your foot down," Scott said.

"You're stressing me out," Jerry replied. "I'll need a smoke in a minute." He hoped the threat would keep Scott quiet.

There was a loud groan from Anton. Forced to lie in the back with his hands cuffed together, he was buffeted from side to side as the van rounded a corner.

"Shut it, hippy," Jerry said, no longer bothering to pretend he was a policeman. He flung his hat to the floor. "That's better."

Scott did the same. "Too true," he said. "Criminal offence to impersonate Plod, innit?"

Jerry abandoned the chase and concentrated on heading for the M1. He found a rock channel on the radio and increased the volume, pumping out loud heavy metal to drown Anton's cries. Receiving the inevitable criticism from Scott, he asked what his partner would prefer: this, or the hippy?

The M1, he believed, was predictable only during the rush hour, when it was crowded and sluggish. Luckily, on this weekday afternoon, traffic flowed freely. Jerry drove south to the M25, slipping off it again to take the road to Broxbourne.

Scott's cottage sat in an acre of land between the river and the town's fringes. It didn't take a genius to understand that it was the property's isolation that made it attractive to Jon. Jerry wasn't sure why Scott had agreed to let Jon use it, though. He didn't think it was fear. Scott always said the lad wasn't a patch on his old man; he wished Shaun hadn't been careless enough to get banged up.

Jerry wondered what Jon had planned for the afternoon. It wouldn't be a tea party. "Where's your girlfriend? And her children?" he asked.

"Out. Visiting her mother." Scott replied. "Sooty's with them." Sooty was his greyhound, and, Jerry suspected, the member of the family that Scott loved most.

Jon and Vince were waiting outside the mellow brick building. There were no other vehicles around, and Jerry supposed they had taken the train. It was a sunny day, but not warm. Jon was wearing a grey fleece hoodie and Vince a black Crombie overcoat.

The Transit came to a halt on the neatly patterned brick drive. Jerry and Scott emerged. "We got him," Jerry said.

"What happened to you?" Vince asked Scott.

"Forget the small talk," Jon said. "We'll go inside. Get the hippy out."

Bruised from the journey, Anton hardly had the energy to protest. Vince pulled him roughly onto the drive and into the house, muttering oaths at him.

"I guess your kitchen is easy to clean," Jon said, as if about to swap housework tips. "We'll go there."

Jerry felt intimidated. The lad was speaking with an easy authority. Perhaps they'd underestimated him.

The kitchen was a large, oblong room with a skylight, a single storey tacked onto the back of the house. It boasted a flagstone floor, rustic oak kitchen units, a matching table and six chairs.

"Sit down," Jon said.

Vince shoved Anton onto a chair, locking him to it with handcuffs and pushing it towards the table. The hippy was almost straitjacketed. Calmly, Vince sat next to his victim, with Jon flanking the farmer on the other side.

Jon contemplated the rectangular, scrubbed wood table. "Do me a favour, Scott," he said. "Put a cloth on there, or a towel, in case things get messy."

Anton tried to stand. The oak chair, cuffs and all, came with him.

"Stay where you are," Vince barked, pushing him back down.

Jerry watched as Scott took a length of oilcloth patterned with black and white flowers from one of the rustic drawers, covering the table with it.

Jon placed a black A4 document wallet in front of him. "I've got something for you to sign, Anton," he said. "You know, to prove your commitment to my dad's business." He removed a sheaf of papers from the wallet.

They were closely typed and looked legalistic, but Anton obviously knew what they were. "I'm not transferring that land to you," he said.

"Oh no?" Jon said. "It isn't yours. You've been borrowing it from my dad."

"Anyway, it's not being transferred to him, it's being transferred to me," Vince said. He cracked his knuckles. Jerry hadn't noticed before how one set of fingers bore the word LOVE, and the other, HATE, neatly inked in black.

"Here." Jon placed a biro next to the documents.

Anton sat, silent and immobile.

"I think he needs persuading," Jon said. He flicked open a knife. "Hold him, Vince."

Vince leaned over. He'd removed his coat to reveal a cream cashmere jumper. The muscles in his arms bulged as he gripped Anton's.

"No!" Anton screamed, his will finally breaking. "I'll sign. Please." He turned imploring eyes to Jon. "Where do you want my signature? Just tell me."

Vince relaxed his grasp and motioned to Jerry to unlock the handcuffs. Without a word, Jon pointed to one of the pieces of paper, then another. Anton squiggled on them.

Jerry stifled a sigh of relief. Jon had what he wanted. Apart from Scott's broken nose, no one had been hurt. He looked forward to a quiet pint later.

"Is that it?" Vince asked.

"I'll check," Jon said. He shuffled the documents. "Yes, all in order."

"Then I can go?" Anton asked.

"I don't think so," Jon replied. He lifted his blade. "My Dad always said the most dangerous man is the one who's got nothing to lose. And that's you, isn't it, Anton? Because really, you've got nothing left now."

"You can trust me, Jon," Anton said frantically. "I won't tell anyone."

Jon's eyes reminded Jerry of documentaries about child soldiers in Africa. They were entirely matter of fact and contained not a shred of humanity.

"I don't believe you, Anton," Jon said. His knife flashed.

Chapter 25.   **MARTY**

Marty passed Fort Dunlop, an iconic sight next to the roaring M6, and knew he was nearly home. He didn't bother popping into the office, but drove straight to Wellington Road.

Angela was in the kitchen, preparing a stew.

"Smells delicious," Marty said, hoping for a hearty portion later. Just in case, he had a stash of Mars Bars in his study to stave off hunger pangs.

"I didn't expect you back so soon," Angela said.

He recounted the day's events.

"Hadn't you better call the real police?" she asked. "You don't know what the counterfeit cops will do to that poor man."

"How's it going to look when they hear I drove a hundred miles to meet a dope farmer?"

Angela's baby blue eyes widened in sympathy, although her brow didn't wrinkle. Marty wondered if Botox was a weapon in her armoury, and decided it was none of his business. If anything, he was pleased she wanted to look pretty for him.

"There's always your friends in the masons. You could have a word," she suggested.

"You're right," he said. He did have good contacts among the police, men who knew him well enough to believe his story. "I'll make a phone call. It might lead to a drink, though."

She smiled. "And a couple, or three. I know how it works. I'll keep your dinner warm for you."

"The police should be able to trace the van and ensure Anton's okay," Marty said, "but he'll be going down once they see his plantation." Even after the wallabies had eaten their fill, there would be plenty of evidence. He imagined the marsupials filled with a kind of Dutch courage, skipping down the lane and into suburban Dunstable.

"I can't understand why you and Erik wanted anything to do with Anton," Angela said.

"It was my idea," Marty confessed. "Erik's still in hospital. He'll be out tomorrow, which is good, but he's not one hundred percent. The nurses say he sleeps all the time."

"He needs to. That bash on the head was terrible," Angela said. "I guess he's on the mend at last."

"It'll take a while," Marty said. "I'm going to give him time, as long as our operations don't suffer. He hasn't been near his allotment for a week. That's the only source of darria we have." He didn't like to admit that anxiety for his supply chain was almost as great as his concern for Erik's welfare.

"There's an obvious answer," Angela said. "It's been staring us in the face since you did the weeding. I'll eat humble pie and give Ryan a call. As long as you keep an eye on him, I bet he could grow as much darria as you need."

"Surely not in your garden?" Marty said.

Chapter 26.   KAT

Kat recoiled. There was another letter, addressed to her in the same untidy writing, on the console table by the imposing front door of 3, Leopold Passage. She picked it up gingerly, noting the London postmark.

Tim was still in the capital. That was why he hadn't been to the casino that evening. She'd accepted a lift from Richie instead.

Could Richie have written the letters? He, too, knew where she lived. At the thought of his large, kind brown eyes, Kat shook her head. He'd been in Birmingham all week, anyway.

She forced herself to open and read the latest missive under the light of the icicle chandelier. It was even more depraved than the first, predicting a variety of sexual acts and a painful death. She stuffed the paper into her handbag.

Her senses sharpened, she heard every tiny creak of the stairs as she ascended. Another sound, as if of heavy breathing, caused her to stop in panic before she realised it was her own sobbing. In the middle of a busy city, in a building where a dozen others lived and worked, she was alone.

Erik's flat was as clean and tidy as she'd left it. After inspecting every room, cupboard and dark corner, Kat placed a dining chair in front of the locked front door. She removed her makeup and clothing, then crawled into bed.

Sleep wouldn't come. Her thoughts returned again and again to Tim. His face, boyishly handsome, loomed in front of her closed eyes. The thought of his touch aroused her, only to send her shivering in fear as she imagined him carrying out the letter writer's threats. Slow dark hours passed, with daybreak dawning just as she fell asleep.

She awoke to sunlight streaming through the uncurtained window. Reaching into her bag for her phone, her fingers brushed a crumpled piece of paper. Kat's heart stopped at the sickening memory of the words written on it.

It was eleven o'clock. Tim had texted to suggest drinks that evening. Her fingers shaking, Kat dialled his number.

"Kat!" There was no disguising the delight in his voice. "I'm on a train to Brum now. How about cocktails tonight? Or," his tone became suggestive, "I could come round before you start work."

She couldn't contain her anxiety. "Did you send those letters?" she blurted.

"What letters?" Tim asked.

Kat flushed with anger and embarrassment. It was crazy to confront Tim. Of course, he'd deny it, whether guilty or innocent. "I've received threats," she said.

"Who from?" he asked. "Are you okay?"

"No," Kat said. A single word couldn't convey the horror of being stalked by post.

"I wish I was back in Brum," he said, sounding concerned.

"You've been in London all week, haven't you?" she said. "That's where the letters came from."

"You think I'm responsible?" he asked, his dismay as clear as if he'd been standing in front of her.

"I'm not saying that." She was suddenly aware that she was either feeding a perverted need within him, or pushing away the one man with whom she might build a future.

"It sounded like an accusation. Kat, do you appreciate twenty million people pass through London every day?"

The others didn't have her address, though. "I don't know what to think," Kat said. "I haven't seen your handwriting before. Do you think you could…"

"This is a matter for the police," Tim said.

Kat shuddered. How could Tim suggest that? He knew how she felt about the police. Of course, he could be calling her bluff. He'd be aware it was the last thing she'd do.

There was a single answer: to cut off all contact with him. "I don't want to see you again," she said.

"Wait," Tim began to say.

It was too late. Kat cut off the call, and switched off her phone. She threw herself, face down, onto the bed and began to cry: noisy, tearful sobs.

Eventually, she composed herself enough to splash water on her face, pull on clothes, and visit her brother.

Erik, alone in Amy's studio, seemed barely awake himself. As he opened the door to Kat, she saw his eyes were glazed and dull.

"What is it, Kat?" he asked, his voice thick and sounding tired.

She realised she couldn't tell Erik about the letters. He hadn't recovered from his injury yet. Suddenly, she felt very alone. Even when her parents died, Erik had given her moral support. Now, not only was he unable to do so, but the tables had been turned. Erik clearly needed help, yet in her own turmoil, she couldn't give it. Half-suppressed memories of her parents surfaced: Alexander Belov, wise and grave, and Maria Belova, arms open wide to hug her children. Hot, bitter tears returned.

"Kat?" Erik was staring at her.

"Sorry, Erik," she snivelled. "Sometimes, it's just too much. I'm worried about you, and – stuff. I really need to move out of your flat."

"Are you thinking about Marty?" Erik asked.

"Exactly. I must leave," Kat said. Marty was a convenient excuse. In her desperation, she forced herself to ignore Erik's fragile state. "I don't suppose you could lend me a deposit on another flat? And act as my guarantor. You're a company director, aren't you?"

Erik nodded. "Whatever you need."

"Thanks." Determination gripped her. She'd seek another flat and a new job that afternoon. Tim wouldn't find her again, and nor would anyone else.

Chapter 27.   JERRY

It was the trips to Bruges that made Jerry's job worthwhile. He could live without the hassle of selling booze, but buying it was the fun part. This time, it was different. He found himself irritated by Scott's insistence on listening to R&B stations, and his sporadic attempts at banter. Jerry, usually the loquacious one, didn't feel like talking. He pleaded a headache until they reached the Eurotunnel terminal at Folkestone, then said he needed a smoke. Grabbing a cappuccino to go from Starbucks, he left Scott sitting in the coffee shop ogling The Sun.

Standing next to the van, Jerry rolled a cigarette, his hands trembling. To his dismay, even nicotine didn't calm him. Nothing could banish the picture of Jon, Anton and the knife, or of Vince coolly dipping a cloth in Flash and scrubbing the kitchen surfaces.

The vampires in the carpark, and even Bobby's fate, were different. That was simply protecting his interests. He'd borne no ill will towards Anton, a stranger who had impinged on Jon's world rather than his own.

Realising he hadn't slept well and needed more caffeine to drive, he returned to Starbucks for a refill. Scott was still there, chatting up a hen party. He was doubtless practising lines for later. Scott rarely bothered to stay faithful to his girlfriend on these trips: he liked to say what happened in Bruges, stayed in Bruges.

Their voyage was called. Jerry gulped the rest of his coffee and bought a third cup. He tapped Scott on the shoulder to indicate it was time to return to the van. The fresh coffee stood him in good stead during the tedious loading queue. He sipped it and smoked silently until the line of vehicles in front began to move.

At last, Jerry drove the van onto the train, clattering over a ramp and into a parking space. He switched the engine off.

"Lend me your paper," he asked Scott, so he could make a pretence of reading it. Having exhausted its flimsy pages, he left the van, striding up and down the carriage. Others, probably fellow smokers, were doing the same. When they arrived at Calais, Scott snippily begged him to smoke.

"That's a first," Jerry snorted, but promptly complied.

On the other side of the Channel, the choice of radio stations was limited. Scott's favourite, based in south London, had vanished into the ether. Jerry chose some French rock music, and set the dial high, deafening his uneasy subconscious and Scott's efforts to make conversation.

They always stayed at the same hotel, a tall brown brick building overlooking a canal. Barges drifted past their window, and reflections of trees, gabled bars and bicycles dissolved in ripples. A few minutes' walk would bring them to countless bars serving strong drink to tourists.

"Six o'clock," Scott said. "Time for a beer, innit?"

It was the first sensible remark Scott had made all day. "Thought you'd never ask," Jerry said. Despite his edginess, Jerry recognised that his partner, the journey and their destination were exactly as before. He alone had changed. Maybe a beer would help.

They walked down cobbled lanes to their preferred bar, a cosy room with masses of red plastic roses dangling from beams overhead. Jerry suspected Scott preferred it because the décor was conducive to romance. He was constantly amazed that Scott, hardly an oil painting or silver-tongued, was so successful with the fairer sex. Personally, he regarded them as a distraction from drinking.

They ordered Trappist beers and plates of local cheeses and sausages. Jerry enjoyed foreign food; it made a change from the pickled eggs and curry pasties at his local in Ilford.

Scott wrinkled his brow. "You don't seem yourself, mate," he said.

"I'm fine." Jerry was surprised Scott had noticed.

"I don't suppose it's got anything to do with the other day?" Scott continued. "You're not happy about it, are you?"

"Maybe," Jerry said, noncommittally.

"Jon's shaping up like his dad," Scott said.

"But is that a good thing?" Jerry asked. He swallowed the rest of his beer and called for another. "Shaun kept the gangs off our backs. I don't know how he did it, and I didn't need to know."

"Now you do," Scott said. "Jon's a clever lad. Because now, we're both in as deep as him." He stared at Jerry as if seeking agreement.

"I want out," Jerry said.

Scott shook his head, indicating it wasn't going to happen.

They drank their beer silently again. Scott began talking to a group of American women at the next table. They were in their thirties, stopping in Bruges overnight before heading to Amsterdam. Jerry thought them rather young for Scott, but they readily agreed when he suggested showing them a few more bars.

"I'll pass, thank you," Jerry said. The bare wooden seats weren't especially comfortable, but strong liquor was numbing his senses. By the time, much later, that he returned to his empty hotel room, his mind was anaesthetised too.

Chapter 28.   SHAUN

Shaun wasn't in the mood to talk. The only sound in the cell was the rustle of his Rice Krispies.

"Ah, kettle's boiled," Jenner said. He made them both tea, handing Shaun a plastic mug. "As you like it, sir," he announced.

"Why are you so cheerful?" Shaun growled. In his heart, he knew the answer. The MP had taken to Belmarsh like a duck to water. He was always busy, either working in the library, reading, or writing letters for fellow inmates. If he was bored, he had his young friends to distract him. Shaun was reasonably certain of the nature of Jenner's interaction with youthful smokers on the wing, although the MP was discreet about it. Chances were, Jenner was having more fun inside than he would have had out.

Jenner evidently realised the question was rhetorical. He sat on his bunk, sipping tea and reading an unfeasibly thick book called "Atlas Shrugged". It was a philosophical novel, apparently. Shaun couldn't imagine anything more dull. It wasn't that he couldn't read; he just found it hard work. Jon was the same. It still amazed him that Ben had managed even a year of university.

Breakfast over, Shaun opened the window and rolled a cigarette. The first smoke of the day was always the best, improving his spirits. Jens was a good sort really, he decided. The MP was providing a social service to a surprising number of prisoners whose reading and writing was poor. Even better, their grateful gifts of tobacco and snacks often found their way to Shaun.

Despite the nicotine, and Jenner's essential harmlessness, Shaun was still on edge. Last night, he'd tossed and turned, dreaming about Meg again. What was happening to Jon, she'd asked sorrowfully.

He took a long drag as he wondered about that one. Jon had been thrown into the business too young. He was taking too many risks. Worse, he was sharing a flat with Vince. Shaun was gripped by anger and then guilt, a rare emotion for him and one of the few vestiges of his Roman Catholic upbringing. He deeply regretted giving Kat a job in his casino, the start of a trail that had led him to Leopold Passage and the shooting that had resulted in his prison sentence. He needed to escape, take Jon to Spain, set up a bar and forget about their old life.

The clang of doors disturbed his train of thought.

"Get down to the yard," Ed Rothery shouted, unlocking the cell. "Halloran, the shower block's filthy. I want to see it sparkle later."

"Yes, Gov." If Rothery wanted to speak in private, the grasping thug probably hoped for a loan. He should know better.

It wasn't a bad guess. "Got any more letters?" the screw said, sidling up to Shaun as he applied a grubby mop to the concrete floor in the shower block. They both knew Shaun was simply shifting the dirt around.

"Here," Shaun took an envelope from his pocket. "I'll let Jon know to give you twenty."

"Thanks," Rothery said.

"Was that all?"

"No." The warder looked shifty. "I've got information that's worth something to you. You need to watch your back."

"I always watch my back," Shaun said. "As you screws are fond of telling Jens, this is a prison; get used to it." He never let his guard down. Trouble could kick off at any time, from any quarter. The best policy was to trust no-one and expect the unexpected.

"Don't say I didn't warn you," Rothery sniffed.

"Don't play games with me, Ed," Shaun snarled. "Be specific."

"Keep your hair on." It was clear that, despite his bouncer's physique, Rothery felt intimidated. "You put the frighteners on that Welsh lad, Tyler Williams, right?"

"Might have," Shaun admitted.

"Well, he's legit. Armed robbery in Newport. And he blew up a cash machine at a petrol station. That nearly caused fireworks." The screw shook his head. "Not the sharpest tool in the box. Anyway, you didn't need to scare him into taking the numbers. He never said a word about you." Rothery paused, crossing his arms. "That's not to say there isn't a grass on the wing."

"Tell me something I don't already know," Shaun said. "Where there's a nick, there's a snitch." His lip curled with cynicism. "Now, if you could tell me who it is, Ed, then why, that would be worth paying money for."

Cunning flitted across Ed Rothery's features. He tapped the side of his nose. "I'll find out," he said.

Chapter 29.   JERRY

They'd sobered up with strong Belgian coffee, loaded the van at the cash and carry, and were on their way back. Jerry was still in a sombre mood. He'd bought cigarettes as well as rolling tobacco this time, and was chain-smoking to lift his spirits.

"Do you have to?" Scott complained.

"We might get stopped, you know. I'm proving it's all for personal use," Jerry told him, stubbing out another dog-end. His usual good humour still hadn't been restored, and he wished Scott would go to sleep. If his companion was to be believed, he hadn't had much rest last night.

Scott was unnaturally talkative, boasting about his conquests. Jerry was forced to switch on the radio. Just for once, the heavy metal had a soporific effect. Scott slumped forward, his head lolling, and began to snore. When he awoke, he was, thankfully, silent. The journey passed without incident.

Night was falling as they returned to the lock-up. Jerry was tired. "Want a beer for the road?" he asked. He'd have a couple himself to send him to the land of nod later.

"Sure," Scott said.

The Transit was crammed with boxes. Jerry had left a crate of Duvel by the back door. He went to open it.

"The lock's sticky," he grunted. "Can you get us the can of WD-40 from the front, Scott?"

That worked. Jerry supposed a little effort did no harm; it whetted his appetite for beer.

"Christ Almighty!" Jerry exclaimed. "Who's this?"

A shadowy figure uncoiled like a spring from a narrow gap in the neatly stacked boxes of spirits. Jerry made to a throw a punch.

The stranger ducked, diving past him and running away into the night. Jerry caught a whiff of sweat and desperation, a sense of a young man in dark clothing.

"Don't bother following him," Scott advised. "It's not worth it."

Jerry was incandescent. "We could have landed in prison," he fumed. "Suppose they'd checked the van at passport control?"

Scott shrugged. "We're going down anyway if they search the van," he pointed out, adding, "I didn't know anything about this. Just saying. He's forced the lock in Bruges, hasn't he?"

Jerry didn't know whether to believe him. He squinted at the parallel rows of dilapidated garages and the strip of stony ground, devoid of asphalt, that gave access to them. Beyond, the rough lane opened out into a road. There was no sign of his unwanted passenger, who had vanished as if he'd been nothing more than a dream. The smell, too, had dissipated. Jerry reached for the crate of Duvel, his fingers curling around a large, reassuringly solid bottle.

Chapter 30.   MARTY

Tanya, a grandmother of four, had been a New Romantic groupie in the eighties. The single trace of her past was a tendency towards unusual hairstyles. Today, Marty's PA sported a short back and sides in jet-black, with a magenta fringe flopping into her eyes.

"Thanks for the coffee, Tanya," he said. "And that's a nice haircut." It was an improvement on last week's green bob.

"Thank you," Tanya said. "My daughter did it for me at the weekend." She placed a white china cup and saucer in front of him and poured a drink from the cafetière she'd just brought, adding a generous slug of cream. "Marty, you may need something stronger. I've had an email from Anatoly Aliyev…"

"Who?" Marty queried.

"You might well ask. It came through in total gobbledegook letters. I had to run it through Google Translate…"

"You mean you still haven't learned Russian?" he teased.

"Stop interrupting me, Marty."

"As if I'd dare. You don't take prisoners, bab. Carry on."

Tanya rolled her eyes. "As I was about to tell you, Anatoly is Harry Aliyev's eldest son. He says Harry is dead…"

"What?" Marty interjected, alarmed. "Harry? He was only here in February."

"I remember," Tanya said, her voice suggesting she hadn't enjoyed the encounter. Knowing Harry, he'd probably made a pass at her. "Anatoly says it was sudden. They're only having a modest funeral, but he thought you'd like to be there."

"I don't know Anatoly." Harry had fathered at least three children with different women, none of them his wife. He'd started young; Marty thought the eldest would be about forty-three by now. While Harry had rarely spoken of them, Marty recalled photographs in his business partner's office and home: two men and a young woman. Marty tried to remember their features. "I'll look him up on LinkedIn," he said. "And then ring Harry's secretary, Inna. No point you doing it, bab; she doesn't speak English."

"What will you say to her?" Tanya asked. "Is your boss dead?"

Marty grinned. "Yes, with a smidge more tact and diplomacy. They were very friendly, of course…"

"I know." Tanya shook her head. "There's no accounting for taste."

"Oh, I'm sure Harry had redeeming features," Marty said.

"In his bank account, where else?"

"Perhaps. But if anyone knows about Harry's health, it will be her."

When Marty phoned the Snow Mountain distillery, however, no one knew where Inna was. She was "indisposed." Harry was also "unavailable". Somehow, it was not possible to transfer Marty's call to any of the individuals whose names he could recall. On the spur of the moment, Marty asked if he could speak to Marina Aliyeva.

Harry's wife lived with him next to the plant. The word "bungalow" did not do justice to their property. It was luxuriously appointed and stood in large, well-tended grounds.

There was no reason why the reputedly shy Marina should be visiting the factory, but to his surprise, Marty was told his call would be put through. The line hissed and crackled before remaining obstinately silent. "Hello," Marty said to the void.

Eventually, Marina replied. "What do you want?" The voice, pure and clear, was unmistakably hers.

"Where's Arystan?"

"Burning in Hell, where he belongs," Marina said, adding with venom, "and I hope you join him sooner rather than later."

Marty ignored her last remark. "So it's true?" Marty said. "Arystan is dead?"

"He died in the arms of that little prostitute, Inna," Marina said.

"I'm sorry to hear it," Marty said, beginning to understand why the funeral would be a low-key affair. "You must be overcome with grief." He kept his tone neutral, refraining from sarcasm. She was obviously chagrined at the manner of her husband's demise, if nothing else.

Marina seized the cue. "Yes, I don't really want to talk now," she replied.

He judged it inadvisable to mention the approach from Anatoly, or the possibility of a visit to Bazakistan for the funeral. At the very least, Marina wouldn't arrange a friendly welcoming committee for him. "We'll have to speak soon, though," Marty said. "I'm sure we'll have business to discuss."

She wouldn't be a willing trading partner, but they'd both have to make the best of a bad job. Marty owned the worldwide rights to the Snow Mountain brand and an efficient distribution network. Marina, presumably, would inherit the factory that made the premium vodka. As far as Marty knew, she'd always been a housewife. He hoped she'd have the sense to delegate the factory management to others.

It occurred to him that perhaps Harry had bequeathed his assets to someone else: his children, for example. Maybe that was why Anatoly was keen to make contact.

Anatoly's LinkedIn profile revealed him to be an oil services engineer. That sounded like nothing more than a well-paid mechanic. Marty looked for a telephone number in his email, and picked up the phone.

Chapter 31. ERIK

Now Kat had moved to a bedsit near the Edgbaston reservoir, Erik had filled his flat with more young darria plants. The pots were arranged on the dressing table, dining table and coffee table, with a few larger tubs on the floor for good measure. Consequently, when the buzzer sounded, he had to choose his path from the bedroom carefully.

Amy was standing outside. "Were you asleep?" she accused. "I tried to ring you before I left work."

"Just dozing. I'd been reading," he said. "My energy levels are low. I can't concentrate on anything for long."

"You must see our GP again," Amy said, her blue eyes wide with concern.

"I will," he promised.

"Thanks." She kissed his lips. "I'll tell you why I rang. There are going to be changes at Snow Mountain. Arystan Aliyev's died."

"Really?" Erik couldn't pretend he was sorry, but managed not to smile. Kat would probably dance in the streets when she found out. "We should tell my sister," he added.

"Why don't you call her?" Amy asked.

"I'll do it right away," Erik said.

Luckily, Kat wasn't at work. Unfortunately, she asked a lot of questions, none of which he could answer. "Come round," he said, in the end. He was seized by the urge to drink, although he wasn't sure whether this was to celebrate Aliyev's death, mourn his parents, or simply drown his sorrows at his own lack of energy. Amy produced a bottle of Snow Mountain vodka from the black and white striped tote that served as a warehouse for items that didn't fit in her handbag. Erik found shot glasses, and they sat on his red leather sofa, waiting for his sister.

Kat arrived within fifteen minutes, in a state of excitement. "Happy Birthday to me," she said. She was about to turn twenty-six. "I hope Aliyev died in agony. It's not before time."

"It was a heart attack," Amy said. "He was in bed with his mistress when it happened, apparently."

Erik whistled.

"I know. He was a sleazy old lech," Amy said.

"A thief and a murderer too," Kat pointed.

"Arystan didn't have many redeeming features then," Amy said. "I can't understand why Marty's going to his funeral in Bazakistan, in that case."

"To protect his investment, of course," Kat said, with audible scorn. "He's bound to travel there soon as he can. The funeral's a convenient excuse."

Erik wondered if his business partner had taken leave of his senses. "I didn't imagine he'd ever return to Bazakistan after the kidnap."

Even in his exhausted state, he sensed Kat didn't have the slightest concern for Marty's welfare. Not only did she blame Marty for her parents' deaths, but he'd obstructed her when she'd tried to wrest the Snow Mountain distillery from Arystan Aliyev's control. Erik wondered if she would try again. "This could be good news for you, surely, Kat? Maybe now you can get the Snow Mountain factory back after all."

"No chance," Kat said, her lips a thin, pursed line. "Marty Bridges stole the brand from our father even before Aliyev got his bloodstained hands on the distillery. But you know what? That piece of filth's death still creates opportunities for me. Without his iron fist on the production line, Snow Mountain manufacture is bound to suffer. So as soon as I have the investment I need, I'll be taking the market by storm. And then Marty's Snow Mountain gravy train is going to stop."

"You haven't got any money to invest, though, have you?" Erik said. She was always short of cash; he'd had to lend her a thousand pounds for her rent and deposit.

"It's only a matter of time," Kat said.

"By the way, Kat," Amy said, fishing in the striped bag, "a letter came for you. I meant to pass it on."

Erik assumed it was a birthday card. He realised he was wrong as soon as he saw the expression on his sister's face.

"I'm going to burn it," Kat announced.

"What is it, Kat?" Amy said.

In reply, Kat tore open the envelope and showed them the missive inside.

Erik's heart raced. Any aggression he might have felt towards Aliyev was nothing compared with the violence he would visit upon the man who'd written such things to his sister. "You should go to the police," he urged.

"That's what Tim said," Kat told him. She stared at the ceiling.

130

"Tim?" Erik asked.

"Bridges." Kat's eyes filled with tears. "I've been seeing him."

Erik raised an eyebrow. He'd always liked Tim, just a few years younger, and very bright. It was a shame for Tim that Marty had insisted he join the business rather than study; he was capable of doing more with his brain. "I'm glad you're ignoring the perceived sins of his father," he said.

His sister frowned. "Tim and I are over. The letters started to arrive once Tim knew my address, so he must have sent them."

"There were more letters?" Erik asked. He flung his arms around his sister. "I can't believe Tim wrote them. He's a nice guy. You agree, don't you, Amy? He works with you."

Amy nodded. "Honestly, I'm sure he didn't. That isn't his writing, anyway."

"Who do you think it was, then?" Kat demanded, breaking free from Erik's hug. "Marty?"

"His handwriting's not great, but it's ten times better than this scribble," Amy pointed out.

"Neither of them would send poison pen letters," Erik said. "It's an evil and cowardly act. I've worked with Marty for two years and I've known both of them for much longer. They're decent men. You should know that too, Kat. You only escaped from Ken Khan's terrorists in Bazakistan last year because Marty helped you."

"He needed me to escape himself," Kat said hotly.

"Whatever." Sometimes, no amount of argument would change his sister's mind. He was feeling tired, a headache pulsing at his temples. "I'm sure you're wrong about Tim. He couldn't have written this disgusting garbage, or he wouldn't have told you to call the police."

"He must have known I wouldn't," Kat said.

"The British police aren't like the militia in Bazakistan," Erik said. Again, he'd told her before. Why would she never listen?

"You haven't always stayed on the right side of the law in England, Kat," Amy said, "but nothing bad has happened to you."

That was putting it mildly. In her less focused days, Kat had partied hard, funding her champagne lifestyle by marrying illegal immigrants for money. She'd stolen her friends' identities to do it, and Amy had found herself married to a Bangladeshi waiter she'd never met. Erik thought Amy had been amazingly forgiving, and his sister very lucky. Kat's lawyers had persuaded police that her crimes had taken place under duress. The villain she'd blamed was dead, so no-one could prove otherwise. Erik occasionally speculated that Kat was more culpable than she'd admitted.

Then there was the still. He'd had no idea a licence was required. Apparently, his sister had known and had proved she'd applied for one. Once more, she'd avoided trouble by the skin of her teeth.

To be fair to Kat, her fear of the police was shared by many immigrants from Bazakistan. In his homeland, the police weren't just agents of the law, they were the law. Anyone with any sense, whether saint or sinner, gave them substantial bribes for the right to be ignored.

"Maybe there are fingerprints on those letters," Amy said, "or the police could do some handwriting analysis and find the culprit that way."

"No one knows I live here except you, Tim and possibly Marty," Kat said. "There's no point calling the police. Anyway, I've burned all the others and I'm burning this one too." Before Erik could stop her, she picked up a cigarette lighter and flicked a flame across the document. "Don't try to stop me – you'll get scorched," she warned, throwing the charred paper into the bin before ashes could fall.

If only he wasn't so fatigued. At the back of Erik's mind, a seed was taking root, a niggling certainty that someone else knew his sister resided in Leopold Passage and had remarked on it. His head began to throb even more, and the fragile memory was swept away in a gust of pain. "Do you have any paracetamol?" he asked.

"I'll get it from my flat," Amy said, jumping to her feet.

"Sit down," Kat said. "Erik needs more vodka. We all do." She topped up the shot glasses, drained hers in a single swallow, and poured some more.

To Erik's surprise, the vodka eased his headache. His memory began to return, nudging the edges of his brain at first, then coalescing into a coherent thought. "You'll recall the burglary in the cellar," he said

"I can hardly forget," Amy said. "You haven't been the same since." She patted his hand.

"Geoff Smith, the burglar, saw Kat," Erik said. "He told me she looked familiar."

"I don't know him," Kat said.

"It turned out he'd just left prison," Erik said. "He wasn't an IT consultant at all. He wasn't called Geoff Smith either; that was another lie. If he'd seen Kat anywhere, it was while he was inside. You were on the news after your release from captivity in Bazakistan, weren't you, Kat?"

"Yes," Kat said. "I had several interviews." She shook her head. "I wasn't paid, worse luck. You think this Geoff Smith's the culprit? A man I don't know and who doesn't know me?"

"Maybe," Erik said, shuddering. "He's an unpleasant character. I've no idea how stable he is. He could have become obsessed with you after seeing you on TV. Maybe he's trying to get back at me by upsetting you."

"Wouldn't he write obscenities to Amy instead?" Kat asked.

"Who says he's rational?" Erik said. "If I'm comparing Marty and Tim, two steady individuals, with a ruthless burglar who put me in hospital, I know which of them I'd suspect. You really ought to go to the police." He put his head in his hands.

"Please, Kat," Amy said.

Wild-eyed, Kat glanced at both Erik and Amy. At last, she said, "Okay. Will you come to the police station with me?"

"I'm getting my coat," Erik said.

Chapter 32.   KAT

"I'm glad they persuaded you to stay, Kat." Richie turned a friendly grin on her as they walked into the night.

"I was just worried about running into Tim," she said. "He seems to have got the message."

"The Snow Mountain rep?" Richie asked. "I thought you were like this." He locked index fingers together.

"Not any more."

"You need to settle down one day," Richie said.

"One day," Kat echoed. "Until then, I'd rather make vodka than babies."

Richie laughed. "And drink vodka too? You'll be pleased to know I'm sober. Despite the temptation in front of me, no boozy juice has passed my lips this evening. And here's my motorbike." He gestured to the red Honda in the car park behind the casino. "My single vice."

It was obviously a well-maintained machine, gleaming in the orange streetlights. "Here," Richie said. "Use the spare helmet."

A man was passing, tall and fair-haired. "Kat," he said.

She recognised Tim's voice immediately. "What do you want?" she asked.

"She's not interested." Richie loomed next to Kat, taller even than Tim. His presence was reassuring.

"I didn't write those letters, Kat," Tim appealed to her.

Richie could have no idea what Tim meant, but he still waded in. "You've got no proof," he told Tim.

"Hey, how do we know it wasn't you?" Tim asked. "Have the police seen you yet?"

Seeing Richie's eyes narrow, Kat said, "The letters were posted in London, Tim. Richie's never been there."

Tim fixed his eyes on hers. Kat felt the pull of his attraction. She looked away.

"Please listen, Kat," Tim said. "The police believe me. Erik told me to see them. They tested my writing."

Erik had no right to contact Tim behind her back. A wave of annoyance swept over her until she saw Tim's pleading eyes. Her irritation vanished. The urge to fling herself into his arms was almost irresistible.

134

"I'm aware these are difficult times for you, Kat," Tim said. "I just want you to know I'm there for you."

"Thanks," she said.

"Time to go." Richie's words were muffled by his helmet. He revved the engine and motioned to her to sit behind him on the Honda.

"Call me any time," Tim shouted, as the bike carried her away.

Chapter 33.   MARTY

The Bazaki city of Kireniat had a splendid Russian Orthodox cathedral, ornately domed and decorated like an artistic child's fantasy. This was where Marty would have expected the funeral service for a local worthy such as Harry Aliyev. Instead, he found himself whisked in a limousine to a smaller church on the road to the Snow Mountain distillery. Surrounded by Soviet concrete apartment blocks, the whitewashed building was more functional than handsome.

"You'll like the interior," his bodyguard promised. In his thirties and powerfully built, Maxim stuck to Marty like glue. The man was an ethnic Bazaki: stocky, swarthy and almond-eyed. He'd been in the police before branching out into personal security. Marty had found him through his contacts with British expats in Bazakistan. Having been kidnapped before, he wasn't going to make the same mistake twice.

Maxim scowled at the beggars clustered around the church door, causing them to scatter. "It doesn't take long for scum to hear about a funeral party," he complained, ushering Marty through the arched doorway.

After the heat and dust outside, the church was pleasantly cool. Marty found himself in a huge oblong space with a beamed ceiling, cream walls crammed with gilt-painted icons of Christ and the saints. The furthest end of the room was occupied by a carved golden partition, twice the height of a man. The effect was more ostentatious even than the shop windows of Birmingham's Jewellery Quarter.

Candles flickered in gold chandeliers, and around the carved oak coffin sitting on a low table in the centre of the room. It was surrounded by flowers too, from single red roses to extravagant bouquets of white lilies, carnations and love-in-the-mist.

A choir was singing a plaintive tune, sad notes floating upwards as if pleading to the heavens for mercy. Black-clad mourners were gathered around the coffin. Marty realised it was open, displaying Harry Aliyev's body. Overcome with emotion, several funeral-goers kissed the dead man's head. One of them was Marina Aliyeva, wearing a long, jet-coloured dress. Her head was covered in a black veil like those of the other women present. As she stretched to her full height again, Marty caught her eye. He took pleasure in seeing her shock, although it was but a second before her expression changed to one of pure malice.

Harry was dressed in the suit he'd worn in Birmingham. A cotton shroud covered his lower body and a white headband had been placed on his forehead. His hands were folded across his chest. Golden in the candlelight, a crucifix in his hand, Aliyev's features were serene. Nothing told of the manner of his demise except for the presence of Inna, sobbing in a corner. Marty admired her for having the courage to attend. He looked around for Harry's children, but couldn't make them out in the crowd.

Marty wondered whether Harry really had so many friends. Maybe the event was viewed as a networking opportunity, or slight acquaintances were putting in an appearance for the feast afterwards. He was still none the wiser when a party of five entered the church: a swaggering middle-aged man and four younger male companions with a purposeful air about them. All wore sharp black suits. The oldest fellow, clearly the leader of the group, nodded to both Marina and Inna, then strode to the coffin to pay his respects.

"The President's son," Maxim whispered.

Marty remembered rumours about Harry Aliyev's friends in high places. It was small wonder that, when Harry wanted Sasha Belov's factory and his wife, he'd been able to take them.

The choir stopped singing. A gate in the centre of the golden partition now opened, and the congregation inched back from the coffin. Marty looked for a seat, then realised there were none. Colourful Bazaki rugs and cushions were scattered over the parquet floor, especially around the perimeter of the chapel, but still everybody remained on their feet. He stood with Maxim behind the presidential cabal.

An aged priest in a long white robe, hair and beard flowing, marched out of the central gate. He made the sign of the cross over the deceased, a movement that was copied by the mourners. A deacon slipped out of a door to the side, swinging a censer. Smoke enveloped the coffin and the fragrance of incense tickled Marty's nostrils. He stifled a sneeze.

The priest stood at the foot of the coffin. He chanted a blessing and sang Alleluia, to which the choir responded. This done, both priest and deacon returned behind the golden gates.

The order of service was similar to requiem masses Marty had attended in England. The key differences were the apparent lack of participation of the congregation and the periodic invisibility of the priest. He surfaced at intervals like a ringmaster, only to vanish through the gates again a few minutes later. Meanwhile, he and the choir sang to each other in a kind of ping-pong. Marty supposed that this, together with the strain of standing throughout the ceremony, contributed a mystical atmosphere symbolic of the separation between heaven and earth. He looked longingly at the cushions and carpets, yet the throng continued to stand. The urge to fidget was irresistible. Discreetly he shifted his weight from one foot to the other as the priest delivered his homily.

The Arystan Aliyev described in the speech was not a man Marty recognised. A devoted husband and father, a pillar of the community and the soul of kindness to his employees, took shape. Marty suspected the cleric had never met Harry, who was far too interested in earthly pleasures to chase spiritual perfection.

To Marty's relief, the sycophantic sermon brought the ceremony to an end. The choir sang as the congregation queued to kiss Harry's cross and headband.

Marty turned entreating eyes to Maxim.

The bodyguard nodded. "It is the custom," he said, adding drily, "There will be vodka later."

Marty steeled himself, making the sign of the cross and letting his lips brush the headband. A shudder ran through him, as he remembered Sasha Belov, whom he would once have called his best friend. He was surer than ever that Harry had orchestrated Sasha's imprisonment and his death by firing squad in order to seize the factory. Sasha's corpse had almost certainly been thrown into a pauper's grave. Forcing himself to gaze into Harry's face, Marty saw no guilt, only peace. Candlelight lent him an angelic halo. Suddenly nauseous, Marty stood in front of the choir, light-headed and virtually choking on incense.

The priest waited until the mourners had finished before reading a prayer of absolution written on a white card, placing it in Harry's hand. Aliyev would meet his maker in a state of grace, the proof of his forgiveness clutched to his heart.

Intoning a solemn melody, the cleric nodded to a group of half a dozen men nearby. They stepped forward to place the lid on the coffin, picking it up in one fluid movement, as if choreographed. As the coffin was carried from the church, Marty identified Anatoly Aliyev among the pall-bearers.

Anatoly nodded to him. He was a tall, dark, saturnine-looking man, his blue eyes watchful.

Marty's limousine was waiting outside. He squinted at the chauffeur. It looked to be the same man, but Marty was nevertheless relieved when Maxim insisted on checking the driver's ID card.

Marty noted the coffin, laden with flowers, being loaded into a hearse. The cortège had left by the time Maxim was satisfied with his security precautions. They drove past the vodka distillery, out of Kireniat and then back into its fringes, looping through countryside. The hedgerows were lush, as the shoots of spring transformed into summer flowers. Marty spotted darria bushes, cannabis, foxgloves and Herb Robert. There were bound to be other weeds with medicinal properties known only to the old wives of Bazakistan. It was surely couldn't be long before Big Pharma took an interest.

Just inside the city boundaries, the car drove down an avenue of fir trees, halting in front of an impressive cemetery. Pale marble angels, crosses and even a small mausoleum were laid out across a well-tended lawn. The funeral party were gathered behind the priest and his deacon, who led the way across the springy turf to a newly dug plot. The coffin-bearers followed, then the choir, still singing God's praises. Marty trailed at the rear of the group. The sun beat down on his bald head.

Strands of Marina's blonde hair escaped from her veil and glimmered in the sunshine. She looked strikingly beautiful and completely unmoved, staring into the distance as the wooden box was lowered into its tomb. The deacon swung his censer to and fro, sending tendrils of its acrid perfume into the hushed air. With a final hymn from the choir and prayer from the priest, the remaining contents of the censer were emptied into the grave.

The priest picked up a handful of soil, and flung it on top of the coffin. Many of the congregation followed suit. Marina didn't. Marty, too, hung back.

Anatoly Aliyev finally made a beeline for him, offering a handshake. "I'm Tolya Aliyev," he said. "Thanks for coming." His grip and voice were firm, but his eyes still appeared wary.

"It was the least I could do," Marty said. "We were business partners for years. I'm sorry for your loss."

"My father spoke of you," Tolya said. "He believed you had a good head on your shoulders. You will, no doubt, be considering what might happen to Snow Mountain now."

"It had crossed my mind," Marty admitted.

"As I understand it, my father did not leave a will," Tolya said. "It would be fair to say he didn't expect to die so soon." He grimaced. "Or, indeed, in such circumstances. In any event, that means that his estate passes to his widow on death." He glared at Marina, who was deep in conversation with the President's son.

"Do I take it you are not friends?" Marty asked, wondering if Marina was playing a dangerous game. Here she was cosying up to the authorities, yet she'd been close to revolutionaries who planned to overthrow the State.

"I believe she killed him," Tolya said.

"Didn't he die…" Marty began, looking over his shoulder at Inna. She was still alone, pretty and sad.

"Yes," Tolya said. "It must have been a slow-acting poison. Coupled with his exertion, it was enough to trigger a heart attack. Incidentally, I don't blame my father for looking elsewhere. Marina was not a good wife to him."

Privately, Marty agreed, although he hadn't imagined her an assassin. "That doesn't mean she poisoned him," he pointed out. "Surely there was an autopsy already? They'd have taken blood samples and established any hint of foul play."

Tolya's eyes narrowed. "This isn't England. Doctors are easily bribed." He gestured towards a youth of obvious Bazaki roots and a young blonde woman. "Come, meet my half-brother and sister. We're going to take legal action to obtain our rightful inheritance. If necessary, we'll get the body exhumed to prove my father was murdered."

Marty doubted that he'd succeed, given Marina's money and political connections, but he allowed himself to be introduced to the other Aliyev children. "I enjoyed working with your father," he said, which by and large, was true. While repulsed by the manner in which Harry had acquired the Snow Mountain factory, he had to acknowledge the vodka maker's engineering and networking skills; his name had always opened doors in Bazakistan.

"I hope you'll stay for the wake," Tolya urged, pointing to a large modern whitewashed villa to the side of the avenue of trees. "After the stress of my father's death, we all need a good party. There's a feast ready for us, with vodka too."

"Told you," Maxim muttered.

"Thank you, but I'll go back to my hotel," Marty said. "I don't feel in the mood to celebrate." He'd prefer to be alone in his air-conditioned room, opening a chilled beer from the minibar.

Tolya clapped his back. "I understand."

"Stay in touch," Marty said. He was about to walk back to the car when Maxim clutched at his arm.

"Someone else wants to talk to you," the bodyguard said.

Marty spun around, encountering Marina. She'd evidently extricated herself from her discussions with the great and good. "Ah, the grieving widow," he observed.

She cut to the chase. "What do Arystan's bastards want with you?" she asked.

"Social chit-chat," Marty said. "This and that. Whereas you and I must talk business. I own the Snow Mountain brand, as you know. That factory will be a great money-spinner for you as long as you can guarantee me continuity and quality of supply. How are you going to do that?"

Marina flushed. "This is hardly the time and place," she began.

"Don't give me that," Marty said. "We both know you'd be dancing on Harry's grave if it weren't for your audience. You may not wish to dirty your hands with commerce, but if you want to keep your luxury lifestyle, you'll need competent managers in the distillery." She'd be well advised to bribe the right people too, but perhaps she already had that under control.

Her green eyes appealed to him. "My children could run it. At last, with Arystan dead, Erik and Katya could return to Bazakistan. Tell them, Marty. Let them know I survived."

Chapter 34.   ERIK

Erik still wasn't back at work, but, with a huge effort of will, he was visiting the allotment every day. Although clinical trials on the cancer treatment were in full swing, Marty had offered to keep a watchful eye on them until Erik was better. Their darria supply was a different matter. They were totally reliant on the allotment and the pots squeezed into nooks and crannies at Leopold Passage. Besides, Erik's GP had prescribed sunshine. He'd suggested rest too, a recommendation that Erik had chosen to ignore.

This morning, the weather in Birmingham was sunny and warm, as it would also be in his homeland at the beginning of June. His darria shrubs were thriving. Weeds were growing on the plot too, and he hoed them until his energy faded. He had just enough strength to cycle home. Staggering to the top floor, he climbed into bed and went straight to sleep.

The sun was still high when he awoke. Erik saw from his phone that it was 3pm. He made tea and toast. Somewhat revived, he switched on his laptop.

It was concern for Marty that prompted Erik to look at the news in Kireniat. He was relieved to see no reports of unrest, kidnapping or violence against expats. There was a short obituary for Arystan Aliyev, accompanied by a grainy photograph of the engineer as a young man. A more distinct picture showed friends and family clustered around his grave.

Erik was suddenly aware of blood rushing to his head and throbbing at his temples. The shot revealed a stunning blonde gazing at the coffin, her expression severe. She bore a striking resemblance to Kat. "R - widow Marina Aliyeva," he read.

It wasn't Kat, of course. How could it be? Yet the only alternative was equally bizarre. He remembered another woman with the same pale beauty: his mother. He'd seen that severity on her face, and on Kat's, in times of trouble. Indeed, as his sister hurtled into adolescence more than a decade before, everyone had remarked on her likeness to her mother.

Was this a picture of Maria Belova? The woman at the burial seemed so youthful. Lightheaded and shaking, Erik zoomed in closer and closer until the image was pixelated. He was still uncertain. One man, though, would know for sure. Marty had been to the funeral. Trembling, Erik speed-dialled his number.

"Hello? If you're disturbing my evening, Erik, it must be important. What's up?" Marty said.

He'd forgotten the time difference. Marty was probably in a bar.

As if reading his thoughts, Marty said, "I'm working in my hotel room tonight. Thought I'd give my bodyguard a rest."

"Is my mother alive?" Erik asked, the question spilling from his mouth as soon as Marty paused for breath.

"Yes," Marty replied.

"Marina Aliyeva?" Erik asked.

"Yes," Marty repeated.

How had this happened? He'd believed his mother dead for over a decade, but for all that time, she'd been married to his arch-enemy. Erik shivered, unsteady on his feet. A strangled sob escaped his lips.

Marty divined his confusion. "Don't be too hasty, Erik," he said, his tone sympathetic.

"I don't understand."

"Trust me," Marty said. "Don't say anything to your sister yet. There's a lot you don't know. You need to hear it first, and I'm going to tell you face to face."

"Skype me," Erik demanded. "Tell me now."

"No." Marty wouldn't budge. After a long pause, he said, with evident reluctance, "Listen, Erik. Promise me you'll wait. I'll try to switch my flight to the last plane out of Kireniat tonight. It takes twelve hours to Heathrow. Expect to see me tomorrow lunchtime if you don't hear otherwise."

Chapter 35.   MARTY

The only remaining flight scheduled to depart from Kireniat was a short hop to Bazaku City. There, Marty would have been obliged to wait five hours to catch another plane, which wouldn't even have taken him to London; he would have to transfer again in Amsterdam. He chose to wait for the first red-eye from Kireniat at around 4am. Having deliberately kept himself awake until then, he slept soundly in his blissfully reclining business class seat.

The time difference between Kireniat and London was on his side. Refreshed and pumped full of complimentary coffee, he'd cleared Immigration at Heathrow and collected his car by 10.30am.

The rush hour was over. Marty hit the accelerator, feeling a satisfying thrill as the engine moved joyously into action. He was relieved to leave behind the M25 with its managed speed limits, blasting down the M40 at over eighty miles per hour. Although he had to rein back once he hit the camera-infested M42 near Birmingham, he kept his promise to Erik. The Jag was parked in the Jewellery Quarter just before one o'clock.

Using his keys to the building in Leopold Passage, Marty strode upstairs to the second floor. He knocked on the door of Erik's flat.

Eventually, Erik opened it. He was bleary-eyed, clad in a towelling bathrobe, his chin unshaven.

"You look as good as I feel," Marty said.

"I couldn't sleep," Erik admitted. His voice betrayed excitement. "Come in. You said my mother was alive. How is she, Marty?"

Hardly a natural diplomat, Marty summoned every scrap of tact he possessed. "Yes," he said. "Do you want the good news or the bad news?"

"The good news, please." Despite his weariness, Erik was animated.

"Maria's alive," Marty said. "That's it." There was a lot of bad news. "I was amazed too when I found out. Like you, I thought she'd perished with your father. But last year, I discovered she'd married Harry Aliyev on Sasha's death, and was calling herself Marina."

Erik's expression darkened. "You knew last year that my mother was alive?" he asked in an accusing tone. "Yet you said nothing. Why, Marty?"

It was the question Marty had been dreading. "Because of the way I learned about it," he said. "I knew Harry was married, of course. He never introduced me to his wife. She was closeted away in their bungalow." He noted a shadow flicker across Erik's face. "Yes, the factory manager's property. Your childhood home. Harry said she was shy and rarely came out. But when I was imprisoned by Ken Khan in his orchard on the road to the mountains, I saw otherwise."

"How?" Erik asked.

The disbelief on his face mirrored the shock Marty had felt when, peeping through the tiny window in his dismal cell, he'd seen Marina arrive. Then, once she'd disappeared with Ken Khan, he'd overheard his guards gossiping. "She was having an affair with Ken," he said. "She bankrolled some of his activities, although he had bigger ambitions." That was why Ken's ragged band had kidnapped Westerners, to raise cash for weapons. "She's been lucky, Erik. How she's avoided the attentions of the authorities, I can't say." Was she moving into presidential circles now? He marvelled at Marina's ability to survive. Her beauty must have helped.

"Are you sure it was her?" Erik asked.

"She admitted it when I confronted her," Marty said. "After I'd escaped from Ken, I went to the bungalow to see her alone. Until then, I'd doubted the evidence of my own eyes. I couldn't any longer." He frowned. "I decided the knowledge of what she'd done was more of a burden than a boon to you. Forgive me." He hoped Erik could understand.

"How could she marry Aliyev?" Erik said, his voice trembling with distress.

"I don't know," Marty said. "It wasn't a happy union. Harry played away. She must have realised he would, yet she took him for better or worse." He wondered whether to mention Tolya Aliyev's allegation, and decided there was no point holding back. "Harry's children are convinced she poisoned him."

"Anything else?" Erik said.

"She wants to see you. I strongly suggest, that if you do meet her, it's on neutral territory. We both know Bazakistan is unsafe." Marty withheld Marina's offer of the vodka factory. He flinched at the very idea of having to work with Kat on Snow Mountain, and nor did he want Erik diverted from his research. Anyway, it was crazy to tempt Erik and Kat into returning to a dangerous place like Bazakistan.

Erik looked drained. Marty was overcome with sympathy. "Go to bed, Erik. You need to rest."

Erik shook his head.

"Then let me take you out for a drink. I'm sure you can use one," Marty suggested.

"Thanks, but no," Erik said. "I must talk to my sister." He shivered. "I'll do that alone, Marty, if you don't mind."

Chapter 36.　KAT

Unlike Amy, whose flat had been titivated with fresh paint and tricked out with the latest appliances, Kat would never describe her bedsit as a studio. A first floor room in a crumbling redbrick semi, its primrose walls were disfigured by a damp stain spreading from the sash window. A corner boasted exposed pipes that gurgled unexpectedly. The bed sagged and creaked. Nevertheless, there were compensations. The room was tall and wide, with plenty of space for her domestic possessions, if not a working distillery. There was a view over a rambling garden full of trees and climbing roses, whose delicious scent drifted up to Kat when the window was open. Above all, it was hers. She'd paid rent and she had every right to live there without worrying about Marty Bridges ejecting her.

She was changing into her uniform, about to catch a bus to the casino, when Erik rang.

"Kat, there's no easy way to say this. Our mother's alive."

"Did you say what I think you said?" Kat reeled. It was impossible, surely? Yet if it were true, it would be like every Christmas and birthday present in her lifetime, all rolled together and tied with a big shiny bow.

"Kat, Marty has seen her. She's Arystan Aliyev's widow."

Shock gripped her. About to faint, she collapsed into an ancient brown easy chair, ignoring its groaning springs. She listened while he told her more.

She wouldn't be able to concentrate at work, she knew. Kat phoned the casino to say she was unwell, stashed a bottle of vodka in her bag, and took a cab to Leopold Passage. She not only didn't like what she'd heard, she was concerned at the impact on her brother. He still wasn't over the burglary.

It was as she feared. Erik was deathly pale and clearly traumatised.

"Did Marty say she ate babies too?" Kat asked, then wished she hadn't attempted the slightest levity.

Erik quailed. "No," he said. "Excuse me." He dashed from the room. Seconds later, she heard him vomit.

Kat wasn't feeling much better. While she didn't trust Marty, she didn't regard him as an outrageous liar either. There must be some truth in his report of her mother's miraculous survival and bizarre liaisons. One aspect stretched credibility, though. She took a deep breath. "He says she was with Ken Khan in the orchard. But Marty and I were in captivity together, remember? I saw nothing." She'd been drugged by her kidnappers for much of the time, and had rarely spied on them through the window. Even so, she would have expected Marty to tell her if he'd seen her mother.

"He wasn't sure then, but he got proof later," Erik said.

"I see." She didn't really, but even if Marty was wrong about Ken Khan, the marriage to Aliyev was betrayal enough.

"She wants a reunion," Erik said. He spoke the words slowly, as if dragging them out of a deep abyss. "What do you think?"

"Never." Kat flushed. She clenched her fists, manicured nails biting deep into her palms. The thought of her mother with Aliyev made her skin crawl. She blinked away tears.

Her brother put an arm around her shoulder. "Marty thought I needed a drink," he said. "I'd say we both do."

"Good call. Vodka?" Right now, she was ready to drink a lot of it.

"Make it a double," Erik said.

Chapter 37.　ERIK

"I'm ringing in sick," Amy said.

Erik groaned. "Not you too," he said. He was already worried that Kat might lose her job. He didn't want to risk Amy antagonising her employer as well, even though her boss was Marty, who might be sympathetic. "Don't take time off. You love your work. I'll just stay in bed."

"You're always tired," she said. "Erik, you're not giving yourself a chance to recover from your fracture."

"It's a hangover, that's all," he protested. His brain was threatening to burst out of his skull, while his stomach heaved like a boat in a storm. He still didn't regret the vodka. It had distracted him from dwelling on Marty's news. As he remembered, the knowledge of his mother's rejection plunged a knife into his soul.

Amy, by contrast, hovered with coffee and Nurofen: an angel of mercy. Eventually, persuaded he was drowsy, she left for work. Erik fell back into a deep sleep.

When she returned at around 5pm, he'd just woken. He could tell she was annoyed; her greeting was muted, her smile strained and thin-lipped.

"You can't sleep forever," she accused.

"Oh, I could," Erik said. "Sleeping and drinking vodka are the most attractive options right now. Hey, it turns out I'm not an orphan. My mother was alive after all. She just rejected me to sleep with the man who killed my father. And another man who tried to kill my sister. Apart from that, we're a happy family."

"Erik," she said, "listen to me. You're wallowing in self-pity. I did the same when I worked in the City of London, in a job I hated. I blamed everyone but myself, but life only changed when I took action and found another job."

He looked away, until she tickled him. "That's not fair," he protested, feeling like a teenager, with an involuntary smile on his face.

Amy returned it. "That was working for you," she said shyly.

"It was easy for you," he said. "You found another job. You had a way out. But there's nothing I can do."

"On the contrary," she said with asperity. "You can tell Marty he has to find someone else to grow darria. As long as he knows you'll toil on that allotment, he won't make any effort to source alternative supplies.

And you can talk to your mother; find out what her reasons were." She sighed. "You've been treating your parents as if they were saints. Obviously, they're not. Everyone makes mistakes, Erik. Give her a chance to explain herself."

A tension headache was beginning to form. Erik fingered his forehead. "I've no idea how to contact her," he said.

"Marty will," Amy said. "I'm going to ring the Snow Mountain factory, and if that doesn't work, I'll ask him tomorrow." She flipped open her pink iPad cover, started searching for telephone numbers, and tapped the Skype icon.

Chapter 38.   SHAUN

Marshall Jenner had achieved his coveted regrade at last, all the way down to D-Cat. He was on his way in the sweatbox, a vehicle often likened to a moving coffin, to an open prison on the coast.

Shaun, the beneficiary of a tin of tuna, an illicit biro and some writing paper, missed him. He breakfasted alone, his cell unnaturally quiet. Soon, another padmate would be imposed on him. There was no predicting what he'd be like. Shaun imagined that he and Jenner had been thrown together as a sick joke by the screws. They'd probably expected the MP to be beaten to a pulp. If Shaun's suspicions were correct, he and Jens had had the last laugh.

Although the MP had been somewhat pompous, and over-friendly with younger inmates, he'd been company. Without Jens, Shaun had no one to distract him from the thoughts that crowded his head. He realised how jealous he was of Jens, off to a holiday camp, while Shaun's horizons had stayed in a box ten feet square. Sweating as claustrophobia overcame him, he reached for his tobacco.

Morning exercise couldn't come too soon. Once in the fresh air, he could do deals and get hold of a phone. It didn't matter that no one had ever escaped from Belmarsh. There was always a first time.

He and Jon had already decided to use a drone to deliver a small-calibre pistol and an explosive device. The bomb would enable Shaun to break out of his cell, while the gun would be wielded either to obtain a screw's uniform and keys, or take one of the officers hostage. It would happen at night, when staffing was pared to the bone.

There was no point involving Ed Rothery. He'd never agree to carry a gun; it would result in an automatic five year sentence if he were caught. Besides, a golden goose had no value once it had flown away.

Jenner's absence made an escape easier. Had the MP stayed in Belmarsh, Shaun would have had to include him in the plan. He didn't think Jens, on a short sentence, would have participated willingly. Shaun would have had to knock him unconscious or threaten him into compliance. Reflecting on it, Shaun recognised he would have had a certain amount of regret.

Furthermore, it was now a simple matter to make a phone call from the cell while locked in for the morning. Yesterday, Shaun and Jens had received special attention from the DST, the black-clad Designated

Search Team who had crawled over everything like a swarm of flies. Since they'd found nothing, they were unlikely to bother Shaun again soon and it was safe to bring a phone into his room. When he called Jon, however, there was no answer.

His son was still in bed, Shaun thought, hoping it wasn't with Vince. He texted the lad, and then watched the phone, its ringtone silent, for Jon's reply.

Jon called just before eleven, when cells were unlocked, a few at a time, for the cons to collect lunch.

"What's up?" he asked. "Is it about that Kevin Kemble?"

"What? No," Shaun said. "Why did you mention him in particular?"

"His girlfriend won't pay any more. He owes two hundred pounds."

Kemble would normally be in line for a jugging, but Shaun wouldn't risk it today. He had more important fish to fry. The gambler was a lucky fellow. "Can you get me out tonight?" he asked Jon.

"What?" Jon said, having the cheek to follow with, "Are you mad, Dad?"

"Jens has moved on," Shaun said. "I'm on my own, but not for much longer."

"I haven't got your passport sorted." Jon sounded panicked.

"It doesn't matter," Shaun told him. "I can lie low. How about your tart's place?" It was local and under the radar of the authorities, and it couldn't be worse than Belmarsh. He'd persuade her to find a disguise for him, so he could venture out. He could travel up to Birmingham then. Anticipation surged through him.

"I guess Carla could put you up," Jon said, his tone suggesting he wouldn't give her a choice. "She keeps her flat clean enough, and the kid doesn't yell too much. I'll ask her."

"You're round at hers?" Shaun didn't know whether to feel relieved.

Jon didn't reply. Anxiously, Shaun held the phone to his ear. He heard snatches of muffled conversation in the background, then screaming and shouting.

"No, you can't take him to hospital, you stupid cow. My dad needs you here," Jon was barking.

"What is it?" Shaun said. He heard nothing but the sound of heavy breathing. To his horror, he realised it was his own. He began rolling a cigarette to calm his nerves.

Eventually, Jon picked up his phone again. "She's gone off in a paddy. Her stupid kid's drunk her methadone and she's taking him to hospital."

"Couldn't you stop her?" Shaun asked. "Social Services will be in there like a shot."

"I know, Dad, I'm moving all my gear out. I slapped her, but she still went." Jon's voice was peevish. "I thought those bottles of meth were childproof."

"Kids get into everything," Shaun said. "Even a skaghead should know that." He'd been proud of his boys' prowess with Lego when they were tiny; of course, they'd worked out how to open child-locked car doors and cupboards as well. If only Jon had chosen a more reliable assistant. In another situation, Shaun would have ranted and raved. Now, with a mobile phone to protect and his scheme about to fall apart, he forced himself to think quickly. "This is what you'll do," he commanded, "Have a car waiting for me at the main gate. Get me a mac and a flat cap to wear, and bring a razor. You can shave my head when I'm checked into a Travelodge."

The prison would be lightly staffed at night, with perhaps one officer overseeing two hundred inmates. Accordingly, they settled on two in the morning for the action. It was the time of night when the human body was at its least effective, mentally sluggish and yearning for sleep. Jon volunteered to pack some amphetamines in the drone's cargo, so Shaun would have an edge over the screws.

It was the perfect plan. Drunk on freedom before it had even begun, Shaun made cup upon cup of coffee to stay awake. As 2am approached, he settled down next to his cell window, waiting for salvation to fly into his grasp. Yet when the hour arrived, there was no drone with it.

Restlessly, Shaun paced his cell, anxious and cursing, his gaze fixed on the open window. Every few minutes, stopping only when he heard a screw's footsteps in the corridor outside, he tried to phone Jon. Eventually, as the hours ticked past, he fell into a puzzled, nightmarish sleep.

Chapter 39.   ERIK

His finances stretched by his sister, Erik travelled to London on the cheapest train service from Birmingham, departing at lunchtime and stopping at every station. He distracted himself from his churning thoughts by staring out of the window. Now summer had arrived, the English countryside was as lush and green as the fields of Bazakistan, the towns colourful with Brexit posters.

It was two weeks since Aliyev's funeral, and the bombshell that had exploded in Erik's life. He was exhausted after barely sleeping a wink. Even with the window open, his attic flat was stuffy, heat and humidity wrapping itself around him like an unwanted blanket. His fatigue was such that, rather than walk, he took a bus from Euston to Park Lane.

The noise and volume of traffic in London always amazed him, as did the number and height of the city's buildings. Marina had asked to see him in a luxury hotel, a tower overlooking Hyde Park. His bus dropped Erik a short walk away, on the edge of a busy road. A blast of air-conditioning hit him as soon as he entered the gleaming marble lobby. He was struck by the contrast with the heat and dirt outside. Taking a lift to the rooftop restaurant, he found his mother drinking tea.

He didn't recognise Marina at first. She looked like a businesswoman waiting for a meeting: bland in dark glasses and a conservative black suit, her long blonde hair loose but impeccably tidy. At the same time as he caught a whiff of Chanel, she noticed him and removed her spectacles, standing to embrace him. Her green eyes were filled with tears. "It's been a long time," she said in Russian.

He couldn't deny her identity now. In spite of everything she'd done, Erik hugged her, the intimacy and the scent of her perfume overwhelming his senses with nostalgia. He felt like a small child again, when being close to his mother instilled in him the conviction that all was right with the world. His legs shook and moisture welled within his eyes. "Too long," he said, his voice emerging as a sob.

"Let's sit down," Marina said. "Will you have tea?" She extricated herself, slipping from his grasp like a ghost. Lounging on the mushroom-coloured banquette, she signalled to a waiter to fetch another cup.

He sat next to her. Amy was right: whatever Marina had done, she was his mother and he loved her. Besides, all he knew was what Marty had told him. Tales of a recluse content to hide away with Aliyev's money didn't fit the self-assured woman in front of him. The truth was rarely simple.

Evidently guessing he was a bag of nerves, Marina stroked his hand. Her skin was smooth, her face hardly wrinkled. She didn't look much older than him, although he'd been born when she was eighteen. Such was the power of darria, he supposed. He remembered her drinking an infusion of its leaves daily throughout his childhood.

A cup was brought for him, and she poured his tea: black, the Bazaki way. "My son – so handsome," she said, pride shining in her eyes. "And how is Katya?" Her mouth twitched. Perhaps she'd hoped Kat would accompany him.

"Kat is fine," Erik said. It wouldn't be tactful to explain Kat's view of Marina. "She's working hard."

"I thought she was to marry a rich man?" Marina asked.

"She did have a wealthy fiancé once," Erik admitted, "but she decided he wasn't the right person." He, for one, was glad his sister had made that choice. Ross had wanted to lock Kat in a golden cage.

"Oh?" Marina seemed surprised, as well she might. After all, if Marty was to be believed, she'd rejected her children to pursue Aliyev's bloodily acquired wealth. "What have you been doing for the last twelve years?" she asked. "Are you married?"

"No," Erik said. If she'd expected a clutch of grandchildren, she'd be disappointed. "I've mostly been growing darria."

"The little shrub?" Marina sounded sceptical.

"I've launched an anti-ageing tea and I want to develop a cancer treatment. I'm working on it with Marty Bridges."

At the mention of Marty's name, a cloud passed across his mother's face. "That man's nothing but trouble," she said. "Always poking his nose where it isn't wanted. He stole the Snow Mountain trademark from Sasha, and I'm going to get it back."

Erik didn't respond. He'd heard a different story from his business partner. Marty said he'd designed and developed the brand; all Sasha Belov had to do was supply the purest vodka he could make.

"He's told you a pack of lies about it, I'm sure," Marina said. "And now, no doubt, he wants to cause a division between us. What has he said about me?"

"That you cut us off for your own gain," Erik said. "You chose Arystan Aliyev and his blood money over your own children." He

155

couldn't look at her. "Kat was only fourteen when our father was thrown into prison, sixteen when he died. For those two years, at least, Marty paid for her schooling. He told me he sent you money for legal fees in Bazakistan; a substantial amount of cash. We can be thankful for that."

"Nothing he did could make any difference in Bazakistan," Marina said.

"Still, he tried, didn't he?" Erik was conscious he'd raised his voice. He lowered it again. "Marty stopped helping Kat when my father died, though. She was destitute. I couldn't provide for her. I was a student; it was as much as I could do to keep my own body and soul together. You could have stepped in. How could you abandon her like that?"

The unspoken question, why she'd abandoned him too, hung in the air. His mother didn't answer it.

"Kat was a grown woman," Marina said. "At that age, sixteen, I was married. Unlike me, Kat was in England, a free country, with good prospects ahead of her. She didn't need her parents any more."

"I beg to differ," Erik said, recalling how Kat had drifted, and not always on the right side of the law. His anger was rising while the tea cooled in his cup, untouched. "You couldn't even stay faithful to Aliyev once you'd hooked him. You had an affair with Ken Khan, the terrorist, and God knows how many others."

Marina sipped her tea, apparently lost in thought. "There were no others," she said suddenly.

"Pardon?"

"Ken Khan was the only one," Marina said, "and he was quite enough." She gripped his hand. "Look at me, Erik. I suppose you and Katya support the revolution, don't you?"

"No." Erik shook his head. Again, the truth was complicated. He could hardly support Ken Khan after Marty's revelation. "We are English now." He was speaking for himself, if not for Kat.

"You're aware, I suppose, that your father was an enemy of the State?" Marina's tone was gentle, almost patronising.

"The police said so when they arrested him on trumped up charges," Erik said, "but it wasn't true."

"How do you know?" Marina said.

Erik tried to look away again. Her gaze seemed to bore into him, as if she was trying to read his mind.

Eventually, she filled the silence. "You'll see I don't have a bag or phone with me," she said. "I'm staying in this hotel, and all I have right now is my key card and my clothes. Nothing else. That's important, because it means nobody but you will hear what I say."

He must have looked confused. She continued, "This conversation isn't bugged, I mean. And you'll soon understand why I don't want it to be. You are my son, and you deserve to know the facts."

"Where is this leading?" he asked.

"I work for the State of Bazakistan," Marina said. "I always have, and I always will. Unless, one day, I'm permitted to retire."

"And?" he felt compelled to say, although he was certain now he wouldn't like the response.

"It began when Bazakistan was part of the Soviet Union," she said. "It was a Communist country. I belonged to the Young Communists, and so did Sasha. It was how we met."

"Like the Scouts, but for Communists," Erik said. This wasn't news; he'd heard it before.

"To an extent," she said. "It was also a way of binding us to the State. And when the Soviet Union fell apart, the State remained. As did our President, although his Communist principles swiftly deserted him. And why not?" She laid her hands on the table, palms upwards. "Our nation is more prosperous than it has ever been, and the people share in it. Bazaki citizens have a far better standard of living than they would under Communism."

"Caring capitalism," Erik said. It was the President's catchphrase.

"Exactly," Marina replied. Her eyes held the fire that flashed within Kat's when his sister spoke about vodka. "If only Sasha had believed in it," she said with contempt. "But he was plotting sedition from the start. He wanted democracy…"

"What's wrong with that?" Erik asked.

"You've always been a dreamer like him," Marina said softly. "That's why I knew you'd be better off in Britain than at home in Bazakistan."

"You didn't have to shop him," Erik pointed out.

"I had no choice," Marina said. "I couldn't cover up his activities. I tried, but he was attracting the attention of other members of the security services." Her composure didn't waver. She continued, "I fought to save his life, risking my own by saying we were both acting as agents provocateur among the revolutionaries. But when he was questioned, he denied my story. He signed his own death warrant."

Erik wondered if he was hallucinating. His mother's ice-green eyes met his.

"But Marty paid for lawyers," he said. "He sent you cash to take legal action."

"My retirement fund," Marina replied. "Although people like me rarely live to collect a pension. I'm not asking for sympathy, but I do ask that you don't tell Marty. He sent the money too late for it to be any use, and there's nothing he can do to get it back. He's made millions from Snow Mountain anyway."

She had an answer for each question, albeit a fantastical one. Perhaps this was how all apparatchiks rationalised black into white: by claiming their actions supported the State, and were thus always right.

"You married Arystan Aliyev," Erik said.

"As you say," she agreed. "You and Katya were safe in England. When Sasha died, I was given a new project. It was believed that a group of revolutionaries remained at Snow Mountain, and Arystan was their leader. He'd always wanted me, and it was easy to get close to him."

Erik sighed. "Too much information," he said weakly.

"We were happy at first," she said. "Arystan was innocent, actually; not political at all. He started to take less care of himself after our nuptials, though. I lost the passion for him. And then –" she laughed mirthlessly, "– let's say he returned to his old diversions."

"Did he die of natural causes?" Erik asked, an awful suspicion forming that the Aliyev children might be on to something.

"Yes, actually," Marina replied.

Erik didn't know whether to believe her. "I guess Ken Khan was another project," he said.

"Right," Marina said. "The President likes to keep a close eye on those who oppose him. Anyway," she smiled, "I'm glad to hear you're on his side. Why don't you come back to Bazakistan, you and Katya? You could run the factory together."

Was he on the President's side? Erik stared out of the window, at London's sprawl. All around him in the hotel bar, and in the city below, deals were being done, lovers were meeting, mistakes were being made. The difference between here and Bazakistan was that, in England, no one was dying for it.

"I forgot," Marina said. "You want to cure cancer. Vodka-making isn't for you. But Kireniat University is awash with grants for research. I'm sure I could pull strings to secure a research position for you there. You wouldn't have to go cap in hand to Marty Bridges any longer."

Erik stared at his hands. The siren call of unlimited research funds tempted him. Yet how could he leave Marty in the lurch?

"You can't trust Marty Bridges," his mother said.

Maybe she was right, but nor could Erik trust the black widow before him. He didn't reply.

Marina must have realised what his decision would be, for the expression of hope on her lips gradually faded. She signed the bill that had been left on the table, for a sum of money greater than Erik's train fare. "Let me know if you change your mind," she said, rising to her feet. "And tell Katya."

Erik nodded. He stood too, allowing his mother to kiss each cheek. Without looking back, he took the lift to the ground floor and stumbled out of the marble lobby, blinking, into London's sunshine.

Chapter 40.   KAT

It was only when Kat finished work that she saw the text from Erik: "Mother sends love and wants you back to run Snow Mountain."

Kat rang him from the backroom, her voice scarcely louder than a whisper as she watched her colleagues remove their belongings from lockers and head into the night. "Was it really her?" she asked.

"Yes," Erik said. His voice didn't reflect her excitement. He sounded tired. "Without a doubt. And it's all true. She married Aliyev. And…"

"She wants me back to run the factory?" Kat said. She was suddenly aware she was attracting the attention of her workmates, despite her best efforts. "Erik, I'll be with you in five minutes."

Without bothering to change from her uniform, she grabbed her bags and dashed outside. Plenty of cabs were passing. At midnight on a Thursday, the night was young in central Birmingham. Kat flagged one down in seconds.

When she arrived at Leopold Passage a few minutes later, she rushed along the alleyway without stopping for breath, pressing the buzzer to Erik's apartment insistently.

"Hello?" her brother's disembodied voice echoed in the quiet courtyard.

"Erik, let me in," she yelled.

The buzzer sounded. She raced upstairs.

Erik's face was grave. He hadn't slept at all, he revealed, as they sat together on the sofa. Marina's news had replayed constantly in his restless mind.

A bottle of Snow Mountain, three-quarters full, sat with a shot glass on the coffee table among the pots of darria. Erik fetched another glass and poured vodka for both of them. "Drink it," he commanded. "Then we'll talk."

Kat downed her shot. "So, tell me everything," she said.

"She works for the State," Erik said, "and in that capacity, she was instrumental in our father's death."

"She killed him?" Despite Birmingham's June heat, the icy chill of a Bazaki winter froze the words on Kat's lips.

Erik's green eyes were bleak. "She says she tried to save him, but couldn't. He revealed himself to be an enemy of the State, as she put it."

"Whereas our mother was a secret agent?" she asked.

Erik winced. "If you believe her." He refilled the shot glasses. "Her account was extraordinary, but plausible. However, Kat, if she was telling the truth, then she pulled the wool over Marty's eyes. Which takes some doing."

Kat nodded. "Who can we trust?" she asked. "Marty thinks our mother is a shallow gold-digger." Her face reddened. "That's how he used to view me too, and maybe he does still." Marty wasn't a fool by any means, but nor was he right as often as he thought. She continued, "Maybe our mother's a liar and a fantasist. Or perhaps she's telling the truth and working for the Bazaki authorities. Whatever really happened, we heard nothing for twelve years. That speaks for itself. As far as I'm concerned, my mother is dead."

"She's invited us back to Bazakistan," Erik said wistfully. "You always wanted to run the Snow Mountain factory, and now you can. As for me. she said she'd swing me a post at the university."

"You won't take it, will you?" Kat asked.

"No," Erik said. "If she let our father die, either at the behest of the State or just to crawl into Aliyev's bed, she would betray you or me in the blink of an eye."

Kat poured more vodka in the tiny glasses, wishing he'd chosen larger ones. "Exactly," she mused. "How clever she was, She knew, somehow, what we both wanted most of all. Yes, running the distillery in Kireniat and travelling the world to promote Snow Mountain was my heart's desire, but the price is too high. I never want to see my mother again. She connived in our father's death. Who cares what her motives were?" She realised tears were welling, and that Erik's eyes were misty too. They'd drunk half a bottle of vodka already. She didn't know if the spirit or her dilemma was making her maudlin. It was probably both.

"You and me against the world," Erik said. He squeezed her hand, and picked up the bottle. "More vodka?"

The spirit carried away her worries as the bottle emptied. She was receiving sick letters from a psychopath; she had no business, boyfriend or mother, but she no longer cared. "I can make better vodka than Snow Mountain," she murmured drunkenly.

"You make the best vodka in the world," Erik declared.

Kat appreciated his loyalty. What a shame he didn't have the cash she needed for her business to succeed. Right now, she had no idea how to raise it.

Only Marty had that kind of money. Had she been wrong about him? At the very least, he'd been duped by Marina too.

Tim had wanted to approach Marty, and she'd refused. Pride had prevented her, just as it had stopped her returning to Tim's arms.

Erik slumped on the sofa and began to snore. He still wasn't well. Kat tucked a cushion under his head and phoned for a cab.

Chapter 41.   MARTY

Marty swung the Jag onto his drive, parking it next to a neatly clipped hedge. He noticed the front lawn was looking trim as well. Angela, having forgiven Ryan for growing cannabis, had put him to work with a vengeance. Marty wasn't sorry to leave the gardening to him.

His phone rang. Checking the screen, he saw it announce his lawyer's name. Although he'd asked her to ring only during office hours, he decided to take the call. If she'd chosen to contact him now, it must be important. "What can I do you for, Katherine?" he asked.

"This won't take long, I promise," she said. "I respect your free time. I just thought you'd like to know that someone has lodged a challenge to your use of the Snow Mountain trademark in the UK and a number of other countries. Knowing who's responsible, I suspect we'll find cases arising in the rest of the world too."

"Who's made the objection?" Marty asked. He felt hairs prickle on the nape of his neck.

There was an intake of breath. "The Snow Mountain Company of Kireniat, Bazakistan," Katherine said.

"Now owned by Marina Aliyeva," Marty replied. "I thought she'd have more sense."

"Needless to say, I don't expect her to win," Katherine said. "Rest assured, I will be filing a full explanation of your right to the trademark in every jurisdiction."

"Thanks," Marty said. "What about the other matter we discussed earlier?"

"On track for next week," she assured him.

Marty wished her a good evening. He was sure his trademark protection was watertight. It was irritating having to give money to lawyers, but as the loser, the lion's share of the costs would fall on Marina. It wasn't his problem if she wanted to waste her newly-acquired wealth.

Angela was waiting at the front door. "I heard the car," she said, by way of explanation. "I noticed you admiring the garden, too."

"Ryan knows what he's doing," Marty admitted.

"Doesn't he?" Angela said. "You know, you could put him to work growing darria. And no, I don't mean in my garden," she'd caught sight of the grin on his face, "but there's plenty of farmland around the edges of the city."

"Good idea, bab," Marty said, "and just for once, I'm way ahead of you. I'll be completing on the purchase of a plot next week." He'd been outbid on it before, and was gratified that he'd secured the land at a lower price when it suddenly came back on the market.

"Whoever works on that farm, Erik could supervise them," Angela said, warming to the theme. "It could be just what he needs. Erik loves the outdoors. Did you see the look on his face when he touched the soil in our garden?"

She had a point, Marty supposed. Erik was the only person he'd ever met to show excitement at a clod of earth.

"That's my supply chain sorted, then," Marty said. "Let's celebrate."

"Prosecco?" Angela asked.

"Help yourself," Marty said. It was beer for him. He'd see if there was a bottle of Two Towers ale in the fridge.

Chapter 42.   SHAUN

Shaun was amusing himself writing a left-handed missive to Kat when the number four governor entered the cell unannounced.

Shaun tugged at his greying forelock. "I am honoured by your presence," he said sarcastically. It wasn't often he came into contact with a prison officer of such exalted rank, a few rungs below the number one governor, ruler of Fortress Belmarsh.

"Enough of that, Mr Halloran," the screw said. He was obviously a man who played it by the book, although he said "Mister" in a way that implied Shaun would be lucky to consider himself pond life.

The man's eyes took in the pictures on the wall, the newly washed mug and dinner tray and Shaun's trim appearance, although not the paper and pen. Shaun had hastily stowed them in his pocket. "We have a new cellmate for you, Mr Halloran," he said.

Shaun groaned inwardly. He'd known it was simply a matter of time.

"It's someone you know," the officer said, and with that, Jon was brought into the room.

Shaun's son was wearing jeans, T shirt and an unzipped hoodie. His clothing was black, in contrast to his brightly striped trainers and pale skin. His left cheek was cut. There was a black eye above it. He resisted arrest, Shaun thought with pride.

The screws left, their muttered comments and laughter fading into the background noise of evening association.

"Hello, Dad." Jon sounded nervous. He was still clutching the bin bag that contained all the worldly goods the prison service allowed him to have.

Had it been anyone else who had confounded his plans, Shaun would have been merciless. He'd have used his fists, and a shiv as soon as he could lay hands on one, to exact a brutal revenge. His son was different. Shaun enveloped him in a bear hug. "Jon," he said, keeping the tears from his eyes. "This is the last place I wanted to see you."

"Me too," Jon said.

"You're on remand, right? You shouldn't be on this wing."

"I guess not." Jon shrugged. "The screws thought it was hilarious."

"I bet they did." The set of Shaun's jaw was grim. The authorities had brought his son to him in order to teach him a lesson, as they'd see it. "You want to smoke?" he asked.

"Screws took my Marlboro."

"Same old, same old," Shaun said. "Here, I've got burn. Have a rollie." He emptied his pockets onto the surface that served as table, desk and dumping ground.

They both fiddled with papers and tobacco, Jon less expertly than his father. The lad started to relax as the nicotine took effect.

"I'm sorry, Dad," Jon said. "This time, I wasn't careful enough. I should have taken a cab."

"You were in that cloned car again?" Shaun said.

"Yes. I realised the filth were on my tail as I hit the Blackwall Tunnel. There was no dodging them. They were waiting on the other side. I was caught in a jam sandwich."

"The drone, the gun…" Shaun began to ask.

Jon winced. "Yes, they were in the car. Where else?"

"Prints?" Shaun asked. This was serious. Possession of a firearm carried a mandatory sentence.

"No prints," Jon said. "Surgical gloves."

"So?" Shaun asked. "You held your nerve, didn't you?"

Jon nodded. "I denied everything, but the Old Bill threatened five years minimum," he said gloomily. "And they said they're on to your racket. They think I've been using the drone to supply you."

"Oh?" Shaun said. He felt as if someone was holding him under an ice-cold shower, repeatedly drenching him. He held his breath.

"They can't prove it," Jon said. "I said I'd just bought the car. Ad in the Hackney Gazette. All the gear was in it. I didn't know."

He looked young, innocent and appealing. Shaun hoped a jury would believe him. "Stick to that line," he said. "And when it gets to the case management conference, offer to plead guilty to driving offences. I'll make sure you get a good brief on your side." The Belmarsh cons were well-informed about the merits of local barristers, who sat on a spectrum from useless to miracle workers.

"Okay." Jon stubbed out his crude cigarette.

"Better make your bed and put your things away," Shaun said. It was a command he'd often uttered throughout Jon's childhood. A pang of nostalgia hit him, a deep yearning for Meg and the life they might have had.

They were interrupted by other prisoners wanting to meet the new boy. "It's my son," Shaun said gruffly, shooing them away. There would be time enough for Jon to find his friends over the coming days. He wouldn't attract enemies, at least not openly, with Shaun's powerful reputation to protect him.

Jon stretched the threadbare sheets and thin orange blanket over the lower bunk. The possessions he'd brought were scant, as might be expected when a man was arrested going about his daily business. There was a comb, hair wax, a cheap prison razor, soap. He'd been given a faded burgundy tracksuit and underwear that had doubtless passed through dozens of hands. They'd have to ask Ben, or more likely, Vince, to bring in clothes.

Better still, "We'll get you out of here," Shaun said, although it was unlikely unless the gun charges were dropped.

Shaun remembered Ed Rothery saying someone was watching him. It was inconceivable that Ed himself had informed on him; the prison officer's personal investment was too great. The filth clearly hadn't identified Ed's part in his supply lines either. "Wait," he told Jon. "I've got business to do."

Tyler Williams was in the clear, Ed had said. That meant only one person could have grassed up Jonesy: the jewel thief's cellmate, Kevin Kemble.

Why had Kemble done it? A possible clue was the jealousy in the gambler's mean eyes when Jonesy talked about parole. Kemble owed Shaun money; he must know violence would result soon if he didn't pay, but he was too much of a coward to transfer to the segregation unit and go cold turkey.

Shaun wished he'd grasped the significance of Kemble's debts before. He'd been so obsessed with escaping, to be the first to break through Fortress Belmarsh, that he'd overlooked the dangers before him. That wasn't all. If he'd allowed Jon more time to plan, his son wouldn't be in the predicament he faced now.

Despite the aching, boring years inside, Shaun still hadn't learned patience. In that moment, even as he recognised it, he acted impulsively.

Young Adam Bartlett was playing cards in his cell. He folded his hand, and the other players stood and left, as soon they saw the expression on Shaun's face.

"I want you to give Kemble a special treat," Shaun hissed. He handed over Jenner's biro, which had been converted into a basic but effective hypodermic needle.

"You want him to inject?" Bartlett said. "He won't like that."

Kemble was a prison junkie; he'd been hooked chasing the dragon inside. Men of his ilk considered themselves a cut above long-term addicts such as Bartlett, whose arms told their own story. Despite the badly drawn tattoos he'd had inked in an attempt to disguise it, his flesh was pitted with tracks.

"You know, I don't care if Kemble doesn't like it. When he comes around for his fix later, tell him you haven't got enough for him to smoke. But if he cares to inject with this lovely clean needle, he'll still get a hit." Shaun scowled. "You know he will. He'd never walk away. Make sure you fill it with plenty."

"It'll kill him," Bartlett protested.

"I hope so," Shaun replied.

"Why?"

"You ask more questions than is good for your health," Shaun spat. "But all right, I'll tell you. Kemble's a grass."

Bartlett's antagonism vanished as surely as a vampire at daybreak. His body language and voice softened. "Consider it done, Al," he said.

Shaun returned to his cell. No one would ever point a finger at him, nor Bartlett either if he took precautions. Kemble's overdose would be just another skaghead death in prison, hardly remarked upon by the authorities and poorly investigated. The cons would know who was responsible, though. It was a reminder, should they need it, to think twice about crossing him. "Want a cup of tea, Jon?" he asked.

Jon was staring at the photos on the wall. "Who's she?"

Shaun didn't like his belligerent tone. "That's Kat," he said.

"What's she to you?" Jon demanded, waving the half-finished letter in which Shaun was describing certain plans for Kat in pornographic detail.

"Nothing, but..." Shaun said, unwilling to describe his obsession, barely gasping the words before his son interrupted.

"What was wrong with my Mum?" Jon said, tears filling his eyes. He pulled down the curling pictures from the wall, tearing each into tiny pieces.

Shaun made no move to stop him. Jon crawled into his cramped bunk, sobbing.

If only Meg were alive. If only he had any idea how to bring up his boys. If only he hadn't been caught.

He heard the screws calling out the end of association. Their footsteps drew closer, then the door was shut and locked. Shaun and his son would be confined to the cell for at least twelve hours. Eventually, Shaun switched on the TV, turning up the volume. The guilt-laden voice in his head, and the sound of his son weeping, could no longer be heard.

Chapter 43.   ERIK

It was high summer now. Birmingham's streets were dry and dusty.
Every weekend, Brummies clustered together for open air parties:
carnivals, concerts, film and food festivals. Amy went to all of them.
Occasionally, Erik joined her. He was gradually recovering his strength.
Still, his apartment reclaimed, he spent more time in his bedroom than
anywhere else.

Although his office was two floors below his flat, Erik hadn't been
there for months. Days and weeks merged into each other, only the long
hours of daylight hinting at the season. Often, he sat quietly, listening to
music and reading modern Russian classics. Each morning, he dragged
himself out of the flat and rode on the old bicycle to the allotment. The
route was busier now. There were fishermen and canoeists using the
canal, and joggers running beside it. His friend's allotment and the others
nearby had a glut of produce: boxes of huge, misshapen vegetables were
left by the gate with cardboard signs encouraging passers-by to help
themselves. Erik did so; he didn't draw a huge wage from Darria
Enterprises, and his finances were stretched from paying his sister's rent
as well as his own. He had enough energy to cook simple recipes, which
Amy loyally announced were the best sort anyway.

The darria bushes were flourishing. On each visit, Erik gathered bags
full of small glossy leaves, taking them home for Marty to collect. This
sometimes involved a pint at the tavern as well but, mostly, Marty
accepted that Erik wanted to be left alone. It signified a change in their
routine, then, when Marty offered a pint and said they should drive out of
the city afterwards.

"If I was feeling myself again, I'd take my bike and race you," Erik
said.

Marty laughed. "In the rush hour, you'd win, even in the state you are
now. Let's sup another ale before we go."

They were drinking a golden, hoppy beer that Marty said embodied
the taste of summer. "How's your sister?" Marty asked suddenly.

Erik said he thought she was happy. In truth, he saw less of Kat than
Amy did. The young women were reconciled now Amy had her flat to
herself again. Erik also enjoyed having more space; he could see his
girlfriend when the fancy took him, rather than feel she was watching his
every move.

"I wondered how her vodka-making was going," Marty said. "Tim's been on at me to invest in a premium vodka start-up. That's not such a bad idea. I need to diversify away from Snow Mountain in case there's a revolution in Bazakistan, or there's a problem with the brand rights, or the factory goes downhill since…well, never mind. But my son won't tell me who's making this vodka he's so interested in." His blue eyes so searching that Erik felt under the interrogator's lamp, Marty added, "Are Tim and Kat seeing each other?"

"I don't know," Erik said. His sister never divulged information about her love life, and he didn't ask. "Would it bother you if they were?"

"He's a grown man," Marty said curtly.

They drank the rest of their beer in silence. Marty returned their glasses to the bar, and jingled his keys. "Ready?"

Erik expected to see Marty's sporty Jaguar but, instead, his business partner led him to a white Lexus parked between the pub and Leopold Passage. Marty unlocked it, then said, seemingly on the spur of the moment, "Maybe Amy would like to come too."

Erik agreed, albeit suspecting Amy would have been keener on an invitation to the Rose Villa Tavern first. Marty phoned her. He was obviously persuasive, because she arrived moments later.

With Amy ensconced in front and Erik in the back, Marty took a circuitous course. He veered off the city's busy arterial routes as often as he swung onto them. "Council's digging up the roads," he said by way of explanation.

Erik had no clue where he was. He knew the city centre well, and the spots where friends and family lived. He'd rarely cycled beyond the city limits. As far as he could tell, Marty was heading west, through Birmingham's residential fringes and along a country lane.

"We're here," Marty said, parking in a rough earth driveway. Behind it, a wide steel gate punctuated the hedgerow.

"Where?" Erik asked.

"Our new darria farm. I've just bought the land," Marty said. "Take a look."

It was a plot of perhaps ten acres, bounded by brambly hedges and small oaks. An electricity pylon stood like a sentinel near the road. Marty jumped out of the car, with Erik and Amy following.

Marty, flourishing a key, opened the chained and padlocked gate, allowing Erik through.

171

"It looks like rough grazing land," he said.

"It's been used for horses," Marty admitted. "Like much of Bazakistan, in fact."

The area was flat, with little to see except grass, trees, sky and the electric wires overhead. There was a constant murmur of traffic, although none was in sight. It was a reminder that, however rural the location appeared, they weren't far from the city.

Erik scuffed the turf with his trainers, breaking the soil. He picked up a clod to examine. "Not bad," he said. "Could be better. You've bought it already?"

"Yes. All signed, sealed and delivered," Marty said. He winked at Amy.

"Marty had it properly checked over," she said. "We didn't want to bother you."

"You've done an amazing job growing darria on that allotment," Marty said, "but it's time you returned to your research. I'm no boffin, and I need you back in the office to supervise the project."

"This farm will need work," Erik said.

"I'm giving that job to young Ryan," Marty said. "He'll need a guiding hand from you, that's all."

"That would be Ryan who produced cannabis in your back garden?" Erik said, aware his doubt was written on his face.

"Yes," Marty admitted. "Listen, Erik, everyone deserves a second chance. And Ryan's like you: he can grow anything. You've told me you need more land for darria. Will this do?"

Erik stood on the firm ground, looking first at their expectant faces, then at the grassy land around him. He imagined ten acres of darria, each plant emerging from the fertile earth and reaching for the sky. His spirits soared, as if angels had placed wings on his shoulders. Reaching out, he found Amy's hand and squeezed it. "Yes," he said. "I think this will do very well indeed."

Chapter 44.   KAT

"You look worried," Tim said.

"Erik texted me. Another letter turned up at Leopold Passage," Kat said.

Tim hugged her. "I'll get a private eye on the case if the police don't crack it soon," he said. "When I get my hands on the writer, he's dead meat."

In spite of her anxiety, she laughed. "That's fighting talk. I didn't think you'd hurt a fly, Tim."

"I've got to protect my woman," he said, holding her close for a few moments before releasing her from his embrace. "Anyway, I hope I've cheered you up. You can't be a bag of nerves when you see Dad."

"I'm not looking forward to it. I haven't spoken to him for more than a year," Kat replied, twisting a tendril of hair around her finger.

"Yes, in Bazakistan, when you saved each other's lives escaping from terrorists," Tim said.

"That was before I set up a still in Leopold Passage. Your father wasn't impressed about that," Kat said.

"He'll get over it. You've proved you can make vodka," Tim said.

Tanya arrived in the lobby to usher them to Marty's lavish office. On the point of complimenting him on the décor and suggesting the rest of the premises needed refurbishment, Kat bit her tongue. Marty was the last person she needed to antagonise.

Marty, sitting at his desk, raised an eyebrow. "So this is the mystery vodka maker? I'd never have guessed. Forgive me if I don't shake hands, bab. I think we know each other well enough by now."

"I hope you've got some glasses, Marty," Kat said, "because I've brought vodka for you to try." She produced two small flasks, the remnants of the final cane sugar and potato batches made in Leopold Passage.

"I'm ready for you," Marty said. He removed a pair of shot glasses from a cupboard. "Hit me with it."

Kat filled each glass with a different vodka. "Be my guest."

Marty sniffed the first glass, taking small sips at first and then gulping the rest. His expression neutral, he repeated the performance.

Kat held her breath.

"What do you think?" Tim asked, eagerly.

"You really want to know, son?" Marty remained poker-faced.

"Go on," Tim said. He was fidgetting in his seat, clearly preparing for disappointment.

"Best I've ever tasted," Marty said. "At any rate, the second one was."

"Potato," Tim murmured.

"I guessed," Marty said. "So, bab, how do I know you'll be able to make it like that again?"

"Dad, if Kat can make vodka this good with a heap of old glassware and pipes up a chimney, imagine what she can do with modern premises and equipment?" Tim said.

"The costings work too," Kat said. "I'll show you a spreadsheet to prove it." She'd always excelled at maths. Preparing a business plan had been easy. It had also proved, once she put her mind to it, that she didn't need a quarter of a million pounds. One hundred and ten thousand pounds was still a big ask, though.

"Isn't that Erik's laptop?" Marty asked, as she unzipped the attaché case she'd brought.

"I'm just borrowing it." It was time she bought her own. That was top of the list if Marty agreed to go ahead.

She ran through the figures for him, with occasional interjections from Tim. Marty listened intently.

"I've heard enough," Marty said. "All right, I'll invest what you need. But," he looked straight at Kat, as if he and she were alone in the room, "we have history, don't we? And in view of that, I'll be keeping a close eye on the project."

She returned his gaze. "You can rely on me," she assured him.

"Thanks, Dad," Tim said. "You won't regret it."

"I'm relying on you to prove that," Marty said. For the first time during the meeting, he smiled. "I'll get the paperwork and cash sorted out this week. Good luck to both of you."

At last, he extended a hand. Kat and Tim shook it in turn, before he ushered them out.

Like a flashy little sister, the gold Subaru was sitting next to Marty's Jag in the East West Bridges carpark.

Tim kissed Kat full on the lips. "We did it," he said. "Well done. It's too early for vodka. Fancy a coffee to celebrate? My place?"

"You're on," Kat said, slipping into the passenger seat next to him.

The Subaru roared into life. "Still think Dad doesn't like you?" Tim asked.

"I'm not sure," Kat said. "Of course, I'm grateful for his support, but he was really arrogant. Telling me we have history is stating the obvious. He didn't need to say that."

Tim shrugged. "It's true, though. That history is there. Even so, Dad's investing in us. He's trusting that the mistakes of the past won't ruin our future."

They'd stopped at a red traffic light. Tim leaned over and kissed her once more.

"Let's prove your dad right," Kat said.

Thank you for reading **The Grass Trail** - I hope you enjoyed it! I'd really appreciate it if you'd tell your friends by leaving a review on Amazon, Goodreads, or your blog.

I'd love to stay in touch with you, too. If you sign up for my newsletter at aaabbott.co.uk, I'll send you a free e-book of short stories. You'll also receive news about forthcoming books and live fiction events. I hope you can get to one; it would be wonderful to meet you.

You can also find me on Twitter (@AAAbbottStories) and Facebook.

Lightning Source UK Ltd.
Milton Keynes UK
UKOW05f0357120717

305154UK00002B/135/P